Agnesse was completely unprepared for what Seb did next.

He shifted his grip, tipped her backward in his arms and, before she could stop him, fastened his mouth over hers. Too stunned to respond, she let him kiss her. His lips seeking what they wanted, his tongue taking shocking liberties.

He tasted of things she could hardly name but wanted more of.

Passion, she thought dimly. *A masculine feast. Soft lips but a body that was hard and hot.*

She would've been breathless if she could breathe at all.

His arms around her, so strong, made her feel safe and protected.

Her hand slid along his shoulder to curl about his neck. She arched her hips to press closer to his, reveling in the feeling of being weightless, of being held so securely in his arms.

Then suddenly his mouth was gone. Her eyes fluttered open; her gaze refocused to clash with his.

Whatever she saw there was unreadable. Dark and forbidding. "Now, I think we are even," he said.

Julieanne Howells loves the romance of a stormy day, which is just as well because she lives in rainy North East England. On inclement days, if she's not writing and reading, she has a fondness for cooking. Sometimes her efforts are even edible. She compensates for her lack of domestic skills by being an expert daydreamer, always imagining ways for plucky heroines to upend the world of handsome, provoking heroes. For Julieanne, writing for Harlequin is just about the perfect job.

Books by Julieanne Howells

Harlequin Presents

Desert Prince's Defiant Bride
Stranded with His Runaway Bride

Visit the Author Profile page at Harlequin.com for more titles.

Julieanne Howells

RIVALS AT THE ROYAL ALTAR

HARLEQUIN®
PRESENTS™

Recycling programs
for this product may
not exist in your area.

ISBN-13: 978-1-335-58449-6

Rivals at the Royal Altar

Copyright © 2023 by Julieanne Howells

For questions and comments about the quality of this book,
please contact us at CustomerService@Harlequin.com.

Harlequin Enterprises ULC
22 Adelaide St. West, 41st Floor
Toronto, Ontario M5H 4E3, Canada
www.Harlequin.com

Printed in U.S.A.

RIVALS AT THE ROYAL ALTAR

For Denley, Moira and Richard. I can't begin to express how much your help and support has meant to me. You deserve the very best of all good things. Love you loads xxx

CHAPTER ONE

'No, no, and *no*!'

Her Majesty, Queen Agnesse of Ellamaa, was not amused.

It was not only that her perfectly ordered plans were being rearranged at the last minute. But worse, so much worse, her secretary had announced that her co-host for tomorrow's charity gala had been replaced. The Crown Prince of Grimentz was unable to attend and in his stead he was sending his cousin, Prince Sebastien: not just Europe's most notorious royal playboy, but also a man with whom Agnesse had a brief but unfortunate history.

'He'll make a handsome escort,' Keert suggested.

Stunning green eyes and a mouth that promised all sorts of wickedness came to mind, but Agnesse would not be swayed by his dazzling looks.

'I am not having that Lothario within ten miles of me. And have you forgotten he broke my sister's heart?'

'That was more than five years ago, ma'am, and wasn't it merely a youthful infatuation? Princess Isobel was only sixteen.'

'Exactly. She was a baby.'

Her secretary tried again. 'All you'll have to do is sit at dinner with him and make polite conversation.'

'Make conversation with that…that *reprobate*?' Her voice rose to an unregal screech. Had her mother been present, Agnesse would have been instantly on the sharp end of a withering glare.

'Come now, ma'am. Is that not a little harsh?'

'Harsh? He has the morals of an alley cat.' Agnesse began pacing. The mere mention of Prince Sebastien von Frohburg was enough to make any woman pace. 'And he broke Isobel's heart.'

'Yes, ma'am, you said.'

'My innocent baby sister.'

Keert's eyebrows rose.

Perhaps that *was* an exaggeration. Her middle sibling had always been a little wild, the bane of her parents' lives, and now at twenty-one, had developed into something of a man-eater. But maybe the actions of Sebastien von Frohburg had started her along that path.

'Perhaps we can allow he has changed in the interim, ma'am.'

Agnesse halted by her desk and twitched angrily at the positions of her pen and diary until they sat precisely side by side again. 'Five years is nothing to a man like that,' she muttered.

And no time at all for him to forgive what she'd done in revenge. Agnesse could feel no pride for what she'd done back then. In fact, she was thoroughly ashamed. It had been her lowest moment. But for some reason the prince brought out an impulsive side of her that no one else ever had. He'd made her see red by callously brushing aside the tender feelings of a love-struck teenager, when he could have stirred himself to be kind and let her down gently instead.

Agnesse had absolutely no desire to face him again. Then she brightened. 'Couldn't Carl do it?'

Her nineteen-year-old brother had stepped in before as her escort during this period of official mourning for their late father.

'It's a joint event for Ellamaa and Grimentz, ma'am. A representative from the principality needs to attend, and Prince Sebastien would be a natural choice.'

Of course, she knew Keert was right, as the event supported a charity jointly set up by her father and the crown prince, Leo.

Despite having a twenty-year age difference between them, and their respective countries being hundreds of miles apart, after meeting at a European summit the two men had become friends. They'd discovered a shared interest in supporting youth work and established a charity which, over the past few years, had helped thousands of disadvantaged youngsters across Europe.

Agnesse doubted that Prince Sebastien was equally altruistic. He offended every value she stood for: decency, constancy, service. And except pursue his own gratification, what did he even *do* all day? He'd sometimes be seen at public occasions, lurking at the side of his cousin, or as in the case of the upcoming gala, standing in for him at social events, but really, what else was there? It was too much that Leo's absence would oblige her to associate with such a man.

'Has the crown prince said why he can't attend himself?'

'A family matter, I understand. It must be quite pressing. He wouldn't have pulled out at this late stage otherwise.'

'Perhaps he's dealing with the fallout from yet another of his cousin's scandals,' she said tartly, then sighed in exasperation. 'Are you certain we couldn't suggest Carl?'

'Ma'am, forgive me, but you know what the press would say. That you resort to your brother as escort because no other man will accompany the Ice Queen.'

Agnesse didn't care about that. She'd embraced the sobriquet and had cultivated as haughty and unapproachable a demeanour as she could. It had succeeded in deterring all but the most determined would-be suitors—to her mother's endless dismay. How would her daughter ever marry and produce an heir if she never allowed a man close?

Agnesse wanted children. Of course she did. But she wasn't just choosing a husband for herself; she was choosing a prince for her country. She must find a man who'd be drawn to the role first and the woman second; who'd care about serving her people, not his own pleasures.

Deep down, hidden away in a corner of her heart, she yearned to experience what her parents had had. The joys of a love match. She remembered how her mother lit up around her husband, and her father's gaze restlessly seeking out his queen wherever she was in a room. Then their eyes would meet and hold, as if not another soul existed. In a world where most of her life was public property, how Agnesse longed for such precious moments of true intimacy.

But she couldn't afford to let her heart rule her head. She was Ellamaa's first ever queen by succession. Before her birth the law had been changed so the firstborn would inherit the throne regardless of sex. The Toivonens were a fecund line, blessed with sons in every generation, so even with that recent amendment, she was the first female monarch to rule. The weight of history sat doubly heavy on her shoulders and she had much to prove. The eyes of her countrymen were upon her and some of them were expecting her to fail. Not least of whom was her prime minister, a stalwart of her father's who'd nevertheless voted against the new law of succession. After her father's death he'd practically told her not to worry her pretty little head and to leave all the hard work to him and her government.

That wasn't how her beloved papa had raised her. He'd believed she could be queen as he had been king. A true figurehead for Ellamaa. She would not fail the trust he'd put in her.

He'd also believed she would find a partner willing to take on the role of consort to a queen. For love of *who* she was and not *what* she was. Someone she could love in return. In that belief she had much less faith. How could it be when none of the men she met made her *feel* anything?

Once she'd thought herself in love. She'd even said a breathless 'yes' to Eerik's marriage proposal. The twenty-two-year-old scion of a banking dynasty had been charming and attentive, and she'd thought he was *the one*. How foolish she'd been. Young, green, and foolish. She'd been nineteen then, and though she was only twenty-five now, it already felt like a lifetime ago.

She'd even given herself to him, but it had been awkward, swiftly over, and surprisingly painful. Eerik had told her that she just needed to relax and it would be better next time. But before there was a *next time*, he'd discovered the realities of his role as her husband. That he'd always walk a pace behind her, always play second fiddle to her and, while he'd be granted the honorary title of prince, he would never be king, never have any real power.

So he'd ended their relationship. Saying she was 'borderline OCD and frigid' anyway and that there were no compensations worth sticking around for. In an infamous TV interview he'd repeated that phrase publicly, claiming that the split was all her fault, that despite appearances he'd discovered she was only beautiful on the outside and, almost tearfully, went on to paint her as difficult and cold. His comments had never been contradicted. Palace policy was to remain silent on such personal matters.

For Agnesse, it had been devastating. Eerik hadn't wanted her, after all. Just a royal title and the power it might grant him. And more hurtful still was the anguish of what he'd claimed. Oh, not the OCD remark. She knew that was incorrect. She had high standards and liked order. How else did you get through a packed work schedule?

But he'd said that she was frigid. Was it true? If it was, she feared there was even less chance now of her finding love.

Her beloved papa had tried to counsel and console her, wrapping her in his arms and dismissing the young man as an opportunist and utterly beneath her. How lucky they were, he'd said, that Eerik had revealed his true colours before any official engagement had been announced. She was young. She had all the time in the world to find her mate. A good man waited out there, he reassured her, and she'd find him when the time was right.

But Agnesse had never got past the hurt, or the fear of getting hurt—and humiliated—again. She'd spurned the advances of every man since Eerik. It hadn't been hard. None had attracted her.

So be it. She wasn't Isobel. Perhaps men were never going to fascinate her in the same way.

But before Eerik there was someone, a quiet voice taunted her, *the prince*...

Him? That had meant nothing. One afternoon of

silly infatuation, at the end of which he'd brutally crushed any dreams before they'd really begun.

It had been Speech Day at her school and as Head Girl, she was giving the end-of-year address. She'd waited nervously at the side of the stage. Prince Georg von Frohburg was presenting the awards and he'd brought his younger son with him. Prince Sebastien had been seated in the front row of the audience. Perhaps he'd seen her anxiety because he'd winked at her and somehow settled her nerves. When she'd finished her speech, she'd caught his eye. He'd joined in the applause, raising his hands higher in salute, as if he thought she'd done well.

At the reception afterwards, her gaze had been drawn over and over to Sebastien. There'd been something so arresting about his handsome face. And then, while she'd been gazing at him, he'd looked up and his expression had grown softer, warmer, and he'd smiled. Just for her. Agnesse had never experienced anything like it. She'd been standing in a pool of sunshine but it was the warmth of that glorious smile that had filled her with heat. Instinctively, she'd sent an unrestrained smile back at him. A moment of stunning intimacy in that crowded room and her heart had fluttered in her chest. Then his attention had been pulled back by a fellow guest, and their moment was over.

But afterwards, unobserved by either of them, she'd overheard the prince talking with his father as they left.

'You're mistaken,' he'd said. 'I have no interest in the girl. She might be a pretty face, but as that speech just proved, intellectually she's not, nor ever could be, in my league. God help Ellamaa when she's queen.'

Those smiles, that intimate look, that beguiling moment of connection? They'd been nothing but a cruel lie.

Her secretary cleared his throat, drawing her back from her bitter memories.

'Ma'am, why not look at this another way,' he said. 'Imagine how it will appear if you are escorted by Europe's most celebrated ladies' man and you make it appear as if he were dangling after you.'

'Why on earth would I want that?' she asked. Keert had served her father faithfully for twenty years. He'd served her well for the past nine months and she valued his counsel, but that suggestion was ludicrous.

'For the sweet revenge of being one of the few women to ever say no,' he pronounced with an enigmatic smile.

She studied Keert's face, which gazed back serenely. She could read nothing there. He was the consummate courtier. He might simply be using his skills to gain her agreement for something he knew was unavoidable anyway—or he might actually have a point.

Further revenge on the prince would feel rather... satisfying. Whether he was dangling after her or not, if she was as publicly disdainful as politeness would allow, the press would do the rest. They'd love the story.

The Ice Queen resists the irresistible charmer.

Yes, that had a certain ring to it and would deliver up more retribution on Isobel's behalf. And for that other, older, and even more personal incident. Which he'd probably forgotten anyway.

Agnesse never had, never would.

As the charity supported young people, her father had thought a younger Toivonen should co-host the actual gala, and Agnesse had done so for the past four years. This time it was being held in Vienna. It would be her first royal engagement outside Ellamaa since she'd become queen.

Grief knotted in her chest. Last year her beloved father had still been alive. But then came the heart attack, when one night, completely without warning, he'd collapsed in his rooms. Gone before he'd even hit the floor.

Her precious papa, who had been steadily preparing her for this role, when they both thought she'd have another twenty years at least before she would step into it.

Of all the people she'd have wanted as escort for this first gala without him, Sebastien von Frohburg was at the bottom of her list. Scrub that. He wouldn't have been on her list at all. Such was her aversion to the man.

Absurdly handsome, charming, rich—and titled,

of course—the prince got any woman he wanted. He just didn't want them for long. Broken hearts and shattered dreams lay like so much debris in his wake.

And scandal was never far behind. Oh, the salacious stories about him. Agnesse supposed she should be grateful Isobel had once been too young for him, and now that she was not, that her tastes had switched from aristocrats to trashy rock stars and fast-living sportsmen. Creating her own scandals to rival the prince's. Their mother despaired.

'Ah. That's unexpected,' Keert said, frowning at a notification on his tablet. 'The Comtesse d'Onzain has just appeared on the guest list.'

Oh, that was just marvellous. Europe's biggest female flirt in the same room as its most celebrated royal playboy. Could it get any worse?

'And…um…' Keert shot his queen a swift glance. 'Both her daughters.'

'What?' Shocked into completely forgetting her manners, Agnesse wrenched the tablet from her secretary's hand. She stared in horror at the confirmation right there in black-and-white. 'All three of them. And the prince. Under one roof?'

Keert made a sympathetic face while Agnesse sank into a seat.

Just her luck that the comtesse had chosen this year for her first attendance at the gala. Where she went invariably so did her two girls, and the story was that her new co-host had once taken all three of them to bed. Satisfying each of them in turn in the space of a single debauched weekend. One might almost admire the man's stamina—if his behaviour wasn't so thoroughly reprehensible.

'Might I be required to referee a cat fight when the d'Onzains set eyes on him?' Agnesse said caustically.

'I'm sure that won't be the case. I understand their relationship is most amicable. I doubt it will come to...er...actual blows,' her secretary added.

'Thank you for that grain of comfort.' Agnesse dropped her head into her hands. 'I suppose it's too late to cry off and send my mother instead?'

Keert's silence was answer enough.

Agnesse gave herself a shake. Really, why was she worrying? The prince had probably forgotten all about their altercation. A man of his predilections would be more focused on the rich female pickings he'd find at the gala. The guest list read like a who's who of European society. Including the comtesse and her daughters. At the implications of her co-host and those three women being together, Agnesse's heart gave a worrying thud. But she breathed through it as she'd taught herself to do and the anxiety quickly subsided, with Keert none the wiser.

No, wherever the prince was right now she would probably be the last person on his mind. He was more than likely delighted to be asked, and already breaking out his best tux and practising his smoothest one-liners in anticipation of a successful night of seduction.

'Spend an evening with Agnesse Toivonen? That termagant? When hell freezes over!'

The roared answer reverberated round the office of the Crown Prince of Grimentz, and was so unlike the usual laid-back manner of Prince Sebastien von Frohburg that the other occupants of the room stilled.

'Come now, she's not that bad,' said his cousin Leo, the crown prince himself, and the one asking the impossible favour. 'Apart from that single…ah… unfortunate incident, she's been a model of propriety.'

Seb was having none of it.

'Don't you remember her insults? She branded me a louse, and so beneath her and her family as to be unfit to even wipe their shoes.'

Seb stopped abruptly, breathing in hard. Those comments had stung. For so many reasons they had stung deeply.

'That was just the media. We don't know that she said those things precisely,' Leo ventured.

'No, but we know she punched me.' Seb jabbed a finger at a small, silvery scar on his jaw. 'Gave me a right hook while she was wearing her royal signet ring. The thing was practically a knuckle duster. I'm scarred for life, yet still you expect me to socialise with her. I can't believe you've asked me. How could you ask me?'

'Violetta's pregnant.'

Instantly, the fight went out of Sebastien. It was the one name his cousin could invoke that would stop any Grimentzian in their tracks.

Violetta. Leo's wife of two years. From road sweepers to society mavens, to Leo's picky valet—who didn't like anybody and who slanted Seb a pleading look now—she was adored by everyone. Seb was no exception. He'd throw himself in the path of stampeding elephants for her.

Elfin Violetta, who'd suffered two miscarriages in the past two years and whose every desire had now distilled down to just one—giving her beloved husband an heir. Otherwise, Max, Seb's older half brother, would inherit the throne, making Seb second in line, and that was the last thing anyone wanted. Certainly not him. And, as his father had once made abundantly clear, neither would the people of Grimentz.

They won't want you, boy. They never will. And what's more, they don't need you. They have Leo. They have Max. There's nothing you have they could possibly want.

Abuse came in many forms. A father telling his only son he had no worth was only one. But that had been enough to forge Seb's view forever. The people were probably praying for the day their crown prince had children of his own. Pushing the stain of Seb further down the line of succession. He'd never been prepared to test the truth of that. His wider family had rejected him—except for Leo—

and his own father had barely tolerated him. Why would the people be any different?

Seb slammed the door shut on those thoughts.

'How far along do you think she is?' he asked.

'My guess would be about three months. But she hasn't told me yet. I think she's planning to do it tonight.'

Today was the anniversary of Leo and Violetta's first botched wedding attempt when she had fled in her wedding dress. They'd been two strangers contracted to an arranged, loveless marriage when, oh the irony, they'd actually fallen in love.

'She's given the staff the night off and she's cooking dinner,' Leo said. 'Her specialty, spaghetti al pomodoro.'

Seb's brow lowered. 'You're asking me to abase myself before the world because of a menu choice?'

'She only cooks when she has something important to tell me.'

'You know that right hook will be all over the press again,' Seb said, running a hand across his jaw.

Leo grimaced. 'I know what I'm asking. I know it will be tough, and I wouldn't ask this of you under any other circumstances. But if Violetta tells me tonight, I don't want to leave her alone tomorrow. You know how she'll be.'

Yes, Seb knew exactly how she'd be. Stoic on the outside but inside she'd be falling apart. His cousin would be strong for the two of them and how he did that, Seb couldn't fathom. His blood ran cold at the thought of what could happen. Leo had an example standing before him of exactly how badly a pregnancy could end. Seb had never known his mother. She'd died giving birth to him. Which was one of the reasons why he would never lose his heart, never marry. How would he live with the fear or the guilt if things went wrong? As they could, so easily.

But he couldn't say no to Leo's request. Seb never let him down. The man had been like a brother to him, helping Seb carve out some kind of place in the world when the rest of his family couldn't have cared less. All because his father had had the temerity to divorce his first wife of impeccable lineage, and then gone on to commit the unpardonable sin of falling head over heels in love with his secretary, marrying her and producing a son. He may be a prince but to the von Frohburgs, Seb would always be the son of the help and never accepted by them. Since Leo's marriage, Seb had had more of a relationship with Max, but even that had been due to Leo's efforts.

He owed Leo—big time. So he'd do it. Spend an evening with his nemesis: Queen Agnesse of Ellamaa.

Such a pretty, fairy-sounding name for a woman who was anything but! Not that she wasn't beautiful. She was, extraordinarily so. Fine-boned, blue-eyed, with hair like spun gold. A man could lose sleep over her, and many had. Her former fiancé for one. He'd publicly choked back tears when he'd announced the end of his engagement to the then crown princess. Irreconcilable differences, he'd said.

The palace had been entirely tight-lipped on the matter. But it hadn't stopped the press extrapolating, even going so far as to dub her the Ice Queen, particularly after Eerik had given an exclusive interview to a major TV network and hinted that the princess was 'hard to please'. Whatever the truth of it, Seb considered that interview, and its revelations, was not the act of a gentleman.

He was less inclined to be sympathetic when, two months later, the crown princess had landed her fist on Seb's jaw.

Perhaps Eerik had decamped when he discovered Agnesse Toivonen had a tendency to get punchy. Though so far as anyone knew, Seb had been the only one on the receiving end of that. She'd been a model of propriety since then. And after her father's death, she'd comported herself with great dignity in the face of her country's grief and her own. The king had been an exemplary monarch and well beloved and, while it was a constitutional monarchy, Ellamaa had definitely thrived with him on the throne. His daughter had quite an act to follow.

His daughter, the renowned beauty.

Seb had no trouble attracting beautiful women to his side. Never had. He had no desire to get entangled with an innocent-sounding witch like the Queen of Ellamaa.

Even if once, on a golden afternoon, she had stood in a halo of sunshine and so bewitched him he'd thought he was gazing at an angel.

An angel who, regardless of his own title, was way out of his reach—as his father had bluntly pointed out at the time. Because, despite Seb's royal status, he was only the second son of a second son. In contrast, Agnesse was descended from royalty on both sides and from birth had been heir to the throne of an ancient kingdom.

Above him in every way.

Seb shoved his hands in his pockets and scowled at the view from Leo's windows. Lucky for him, then, that the angel had later proved herself to be a quick-tempered devil and the illusion had shattered.

'Have you considered your problem is that you actually like the woman?' Leo said into the silence.

Seb's jaw fell open. '*Like* her? Married life has addled your brain. You may be happily loved up but that's because Violetta is adorable. As I recall, she never accused you of being beneath her, and then socked you in the jaw.'

Leo's expression was one of sympathy and indulgence. Neither of which Sebastien could stomach right then. But he'd attend this event because he owed his cousin. He'd be polite; he'd be charming. As for the rest of it, he'd be keeping his distance and interacting as little as possible with the woman.

He hoped she'd do the same. Then, unlike at their last meeting, he and the queen could get through the evening with no drama and certainly no repercussions.

CHAPTER TWO

EARLIER THAT AFTERNOON there had been an ominous thunderstorm in Vienna, but the gods had been kind and the skies had cleared. With the setting sun as its backdrop, the facade of the hotel appeared gilded by the floodlights trained on every floor. Above the former palace, once home to a Hapsburg prince, flew the Austrian triband, while to its left and right fluttered the flags of Ellamaa and Grimentz. In honour of tonight's illustrious visitors, the grand Viennese hotel had laid on a dazzling welcome.

As the senior royal at the gala, Agnesse was the last to arrive, which meant that, as she stepped from her car, Prince Sebastien was already waiting for her at the top of the entrance stairs. She was obliged to suffer his scrutiny as she ascended the red carpet amidst the flash of cameras and cheers of gathered well-wishers. She kept her attention on the hotel manager, who was formally welcoming her.

Agnesse was accustomed to the impact she had on people. It embarrassed her but she knew she was considered beautiful, and that this sometimes threw even the most experienced of staff. She took time to settle the blushing, stammering hotel manager now. For herself, it also delayed the moment when she would have to look the prince in the face again.

From the earliest days her father had tutored her on how to behave at such events. 'Smile and be gracious,' he'd said. 'It is up to you to put others at ease.' He'd been a careful and thorough teacher, and she'd studied hard. No one would have guessed at her inner turmoil as she climbed the steps towards the waiting prince. To all those observing she would appear serene, composed, the very image of royal dignity, while in reality she was singularly aware that up ahead a pair of intense green eyes watched her every move.

Though she always prepared carefully for any event, she'd taken particular care with dressing that evening. Her gown was perfect. In a soft mink colour, it had a fitted lace bodice that skimmed her collarbone and close-fitting three-quarter-length sleeves. The skirt was layer upon layer of toning chiffon that fell to her toes. She'd chosen to wear little adornment. Just a pair of diamond and pearl drop earrings—her father's last gift to her—and the gold mourning medal for him, that she and all her entourage wore, secured high up on her shoulder with a black ribbon. She resisted the urge to seek the comfort of touching her fingers to it.

She could do this.

A little mingling at a predinner reception, where she would deliver the speech she'd written days ago and practised until she was word-perfect. Then dinner. What was so hard about that?

As she reached the final step, she was grateful

that her maid had insisted on creating a more elaborate hairstyle than Agnesse had intended.

'I know we're still in mourning, but this strikes the perfect note between sombre and sexy,' Dorel had said, pinning a final curl of her blond up-do. 'The prince will be struck dumb.'

'I can but hope…' Agnesse thought desperately as a pair of shiny black shoes came into view. Her gaze rose slowly upward, along the length of his legs, then to the lean hips and waist. The deep V of an immaculate dinner jacket that emphasised the breadth of his shoulders, the snowy white shirt, the deeply tanned skin of his throat above it. A man had no right to look that good in his clothes. She would not dwell on her next shocking thought. How good he might look *out* of them…

At last, she had no choice but to raise her gaze to the glory of his face.

His mouth was smiling and that mouth was something else. With full, sensuous lips that made her tongue flick out to lick her own—they'd become so dry suddenly. His rich brown hair gleamed in the lights. Cut short at the sides and only slightly longer on top and swept to one side in a quiff that begged to have female fingers run through it. She did not look too closely at the tiny scar marring the perfection of his jaw. Not that something so trivial could truly mar this stunning man. If anything, it added to his allure by making him look even more dangerous. In bow tie and tux, he was the bad-boy prince dressed to perfection and she could barely look away. The heat in his gaze telegraphed that he, too, was liking what he saw and, despite her best intentions, Agnesse was flushed and a little breathless by the time she gained the top step and stretched out a hand.

She could not fault his greeting of her.

'Good evening, Your Majesty,' he said in perfect Ellamaarsque with only the hint of an accent from his native French. She should have expected that. Amongst their many talents, the princes of Grimentz were raised to be accomplished linguists. Taking the hand she offered, he gave a very proper bow, adding the heel click the von Frohburgs always did. They had such impeccable manners, with an old-world charm to them, and despite what she knew of him, it felt so gallant. Unwanted pleasure purred along Agnesse's spine.

She murmured an appropriate response as they paused for photographs.

She couldn't help but recall the last ones they'd been in together. Well, not together precisely—because in one she'd been in the foreground, marching away, while he stood behind, clutching his cheek, gazing after her in shock. The shots taken moments before that had been much worse. A blurred flurry of motion as her right hand, and its royal signet ring, connected with his jaw. Agnesse could barely think of it without dying of shame.

If he was thinking of those same moments now, he didn't show it.

'You are looking very beautiful tonight, ma'am,' he said as he offered her his arm. Her fingers settled on his sleeve. She was acutely conscious of the shift of muscles beneath but pretended that she felt nothing, that she was unmoved by the man beside her. Agnesse had steeled herself for the embarrassment of dealing with a lingering resentment or bitterness, but she hadn't expected that seeing him again would be so physically affecting: the sharp, dizzying sizzle of awareness when his hand had touched hers, the way she instinctively breathed deeper to savour the scent of him.

He was more than she remembered. Taller, broader, more compelling. But seeing him again brought back those other emotions. How he'd treated Isobel was neither forgotten, nor forgiven. Nor that other cruel slight. His crushing comments that were seared into her memory. No, she could not be amiable to this man.

She disguised the barb of her response with a polite smile. 'I'd be grateful if you'd spare me the empty compliments. A man of your reputation must use them so often they become meaningless. I don't believe them.'

The arm beneath her fingers tensed but his own smile deepened.

'Ah, but a man of my reputation is a connoisseur of women,' he said. 'Uniquely placed to appreciate true beauty when he sees it. In which case, perhaps you should believe me.'

He was tall enough that, even though she was in five-inch heels, she had to look up at him, making her profoundly and meltingly aware of her own femininity.

And, of course, there was that stunning smile, which he'd once turned on her to such spellbinding effect. He was every woman's fantasy. If you could overlook the promiscuity, of course. Agnesse wondered how many of the female guests here tonight had shared his bed. If the rumours were true, three at the very least.

They approached a sumptuous reception room. The light from crystal chandeliers reflected in the ornate gilded wall mirrors and across the VIP guests who'd paid extra for the privilege of meeting their royal hosts. A buzz of anticipation raced around the salon at the sight of the two of them together. Even the dimpled cherubs, cavorting on the ceilings above, seemed to pause as Agnesse made her entrance on Sebastien's arm.

The Ice Queen and the Playboy, side by side and with such a juicy history between them. The evening had suddenly taken on an extra excitement.

When she'd attended this event last year with Leo they'd broken apart at this point to work the room separately and ensure every guest met at least one of them. But as Agnesse began to pull away, Sebastien captured her hand and tucked it firmly into his elbow, forcing her to walk beside him longer.

'Let's really give them a show, hmm?' he murmured. 'Imagine how much more they'll spend at the auction.' The hand imprisoning hers at his elbow was warm and strong, and sent such a thrill through Agnesse she couldn't quite find the voice to say no.

She'd co-hosted with Leo on four occasions before. A von Frohburg prince always furnished an event with added cachet. Royalty usually did. But the cousins had that extra allure: charm, intelligence, and both were of course outrageously good-looking.

Even so, Leo had never made her heart beat faster like this.

Breaking with protocol, a guest approached them.

In a scarlet silk dress slit to the thigh and oozing French chic, the Comtesse d'Onzain sashayed up. She had twenty years on him, but it didn't stop her eyeing Sebastien like a hungry lioness sizing up a wildebeest.

She placed a proprietary hand on his chest. 'Divinely handsome as ever, Your Highness.'

Agnesse had the strangest impulse to place herself between the comtesse and her quarry. As if the man was not perfectly able to take care of himself. And more. He proved it as the comtesse's daughters arrived. They crowded round him, simpered and twittered for him, brazenly competing for his attention. Really, had they no shame?

He graced them with a smouldering smile, taking their hands in turn and making a production of lifting them to his lips to lavish each with a showy kiss.

Agnesse rolled her eyes. Had *he* no shame?

Finally, he remembered her presence and turned his attention to her.

'Madame la Comtesse, mademoiselles, permit me to introduce my date for the evening, Her Majesty, Queen Agnesse of Ellamaa.'

The sisters curtsied prettily. The comtesse bowed her head. 'Your escort is a magnificent beast, is he not, Your Majesty?' The woman practically licked her lips. 'I do hope you don't intend on monopolising his attention all evening?'

Agnesse bristled.

'Sadly, I must contradict His Highness. I'm not his date. We're co-hosts. Nothing more. And as I'm not the kind of woman to hold the attention of a…a *beast*, Comtesse,' Agnesse said, freeing her hand from Sebastien's grip, 'I'm happy to release him back into the wild at once.'

The comtesse laughed. 'Poor Sebastien. Her Majesty appears quite unimpressed. Are you losing your touch?'

Before Agnesse could walk away, he caught her hand and pressed his lips to it. Those stunning eyes fixed her with a bold seducer's gaze. 'I'd be content to return to captivity anytime, ma'am. Just say the word.'

She snatched her fingers from his and walked away, joining the first group of guests she encountered. For the next half hour she chatted and smiled, doing her duty.

And if she was acutely aware of every woman those green eyes flashed for, every female hand his soft lips kissed, well, that was no one's business but hers and after tonight she'd forget all about the strange effect Sebastien von Frohburg was having on her.

Seb let her go. Even though every instinct screamed to haul her back and clamp her to his side. The haughty, uncivil, infuriating…*beauty.*

He'd been prepared to overlook the outcome of their last meeting. He was representing Leo and Grimentz, and it behoved him to keep that in mind. But the queen had come at him all guns blazing, throwing his genuine compliment straight back in his face, later dismissing him—much to the amusement of the comtesse—and all despite his attempts to be pleasant.

For any other woman he'd turn his back and walk away. But the Queen of Ellamaa was no ordinary woman, and the truth was she'd had him on the back foot the moment she'd emerged from her car and stepped gracefully onto the red carpet.

For a moment there he'd forgotten where he was.

She'd taken his breath away. Sheer perfection from the top of her head to the tips of her toes and all the woman in between. The curve of her cheek, the little pointed chin, and that mouth, *Lord*, that mouth. If ever lips had been made to be kissed...

The young woman who'd once punched him had developed into a goddess. More dazzling than he remembered.

As she'd climbed the steps, she'd been thoroughly sweet to the hotel manager, who'd been so obviously bedazzled by his stunning guest. He couldn't blame the man. Seb had been experiencing a similar reaction. And not just in the tightening of his groin.

He'd witnessed the infinitesimal falter when she'd reached him, the faint tremor of her hand as she'd placed it in his—that first touch had also sent a jolt of energy through him—and it had brought out the overprotective, chest-beating alpha male in him. It was just as well he was her official escort for the evening. At that moment he could have flattened any other man who'd dared to touch her.

All his former lovers would say he treated them with respect and care. But this? This was something new. Underneath all that icy reserve he'd sensed a vulnerability about her, and with it came the fierce certainty that it was he who must step into the role of chief protector.

How was that even logical, when she had a team of security to do just that, and when he was the one on the receiving end of the attacks? She'd loaded a poisoned barb into every one of their exchanges so far.

When she'd fully raised her eyes to his—bewitching, blue as a summer's day—for a tantalising moment they'd telegraphed that she liked what she saw, but then hardened with challenge and barely veiled hostility. Agnesse Toivonen had not forgiven his supposed transgression against her spoilt younger sister. Even after five years. Damn it, the woman knew how to hold a grudge.

But then the comtesse arrived, flirting outrageously, and he'd seen an interesting flicker of possessive anger in Agnesse. She might have walked off, dismissing him in the process, but Seb could tell she wasn't as immune to him as she pretended.

He'd give her one more chance to be even halfway civil. If not, then the gloves came off. He'd show Agnesse Toivonen that even the Ice Queen herself could melt for him.

CHAPTER THREE

THE MOMENT FOR Agnesse's speech had arrived.

She extracted the discreet bundle of cue cards from her evening bag and advanced towards the podium. Over the years she'd made so many speeches, two of them at this event before, so there really was no need for the churning in her gut. But it was there all the same, and it was getting worse. As was the tightness in her chest and the plea playing over and over in her head.

Let me be good enough tonight.

She plastered on her most serene of smiles and bought some precious time by arranging her cards on the lectern before her, willing her heartbeat to slow and her clammy palms to stop sweating.

Please, God, not here. It couldn't happen here. There were so many eyes on her and as she looked up, she forced herself to scan them calmly, praying no one would notice her trembling. And if they did, to put it down to stage fright. Not the fear that she might be about to lose the ability to breathe, right here in front of everyone.

But the speech calmed her. The familiar routine and the words she'd learned by rote, the question here, the pause for laughter there—it lowered her heart rate, steadied her breathing. And the memories, the things she wanted to say about her father, filled her with pride. Not panic.

She spoke of his legacy, his hopes for the future of the charity, and of her intention to keep those hopes burning bright for all the youngsters who'd benefit from the money raised tonight. When she left the lectern Sebastien waited for her, his gaze burning with concern. Had he seen? Had he spotted her moments of weakness?

'You spoke movingly of your father,' he said, reaching out an arm to support her as she stepped down from the stage. 'He would have been very proud of you tonight.'

He sounded sincere but it reminded her uncomfortably of that other occasion, where he had appeared impressed. Until later, when she'd overheard him reveal what he truly thought of her.

'Shall we go into dinner?' she said, cutting across him. Not trusting his motives at all.

The fear had subsided, the faint nausea gone, so she barely leant on his arm at all and averted her gaze from the shadow of concern she saw in his. He must not see. *No one* must see. The first queen regnant of Ellamaa could not appear to be weak in front of any of them.

Be good enough, Agnesse.

'I wonder why your brother wasn't sent tonight instead,' she said to divert his attention.

'Max? This isn't his thing at all. He'd have had guests demanding a refund.'

'And you, I suppose, will be doing the opposite?' she said.

He sent her a smug grin that told her he had every confidence of that. She wanted to despise him for it but couldn't.

This gala was designed to attract those with very deep pockets, and the event team had created an appropriately lavish spectacle. The ballroom was already a rococo masterpiece, lined with wall mirrors, richly gilded stucco, and a second painted ceiling, this one depicting the story of Cupid and Psyche. But the addition of floral arrangements, statues, and dramatic lighting made the room even more splendid. The designers had taken their theme from the painted ceiling overhead. The stage was graced with a giant ice sculpture of the lovers entwined. Each table bore its own Cupid statuette primed with an arrow of glimmering gold. As Sebastien helped her to her seat, Agnesse noted their Cupid's arrow was directed straight towards her. She sent the impertinent immortal a glare as she arranged the chiffon layers of her dress neatly around her feet.

As Sebastien took his own seat the artful lighting cast him in the strangest shadows. He was darkly handsome, like a god of the Underworld. Alluring, dangerous, and forbidden. Definitely forbidden. Royal playboys were off-limits to queens attempting to stake a serious and dignified place in the world. However affecting he might be. She flexed her fingers as the back of her hand tingled from his remembered kiss.

Dinner was served and her situation became easier. The comtesse, who had been assigned to their table, sat to Sebastien's left and monopolised his attention. He seemed more than happy to oblige her, chatting easily, laughing, and getting cosy with the older woman. Not seeming to mind how often she touched her hand to his arm, or that it dropped on occasion to his thigh and lingered there.

Of course, it didn't bother Agnesse, either. Why would it? She was engaged in conversation with an elderly duke who regaled her with a monologue on his pet topic: the life cycle of the Mason bee, which was fascinating. Really, it was.

When it came time for the charity auction, which was to be compèred by her co-host, she discovered that Sebastien's skills ran not only to charming a comtesse, but also captivating an entire room of people. He had them eating out of his hand, and emptying out their pockets. Cookery courses with celebrity chefs, holidays on private islands, coaching sessions with tennis stars, all went for outrageous sums.

He flirted, he cajoled, he feigned abject disappointment when a sum achieved wasn't to his liking, and the laughing bidders found themselves parting with small fortunes. Agnesse even bid on an item herself: a photo shoot with a celebrated portrait photographer, which she would gift to Isobel.

Her sister would adore it. But the royal auction-eer sent her a pirate's smile from the lectern as he talked up the lot and sent the price higher.

'I paid four times what the photo shoot was worth,' she said as he returned to her side once the auction concluded and the dancing began. She was impressed by how much he'd helped to raise but wild horses wouldn't drag that from her. He was already far too pleased with himself.

His eyes twinkled down at her. 'And the children it supports will be grateful.'

She softened. 'Of course, I don't begrudge a cent of it. I know how much the money is needed. I often accompanied my father when he visited the youth groups and I was humbled by the resilience of those children.' She waved a hand to encompass the room of wealthy partygoers. 'We live a life of such privilege. How can we begin to imagine what they've suffered?'

'I can,' he said with a dismissive snort, and then his jaw tightened as if he regretted speaking.

'But you've been raised as I have, in luxury. How can you have known a moment's want…?' Agnesse halted abruptly. She'd sounded so dismissive, so heartless, when she'd really not meant to.

'Deprivation isn't only an absence of material things. We aren't all blessed with kindly fathers, Your Majesty,' he said, tightly.

The bleakness in his eyes was in such marked contrast to the laughing man of moments before,

and so unlike everything she thought she knew
about the infamous pleasure seeker that she wondered, did Sebastien von Frohburg have a darker
past than appearances would suggest? Had she just
glimpsed the real man behind the fine manners and
handsome face?

He was gazing out calmly enough as couples
began filling the dance floor, but a muscle worked
in his jaw, and Agnesse had the crazy urge to reach
out and caress it to stillness. She curled her hands
firmly in her lap.

That strange sadness in his eyes had simply been
a trick of the light, or maybe she was just being
overly sentimental. The impudent little god glinted
in the centre of the table. She reached out and swivelled Cupid so that he—and his ruinous arrow—
faced safely in the opposite direction.

When she sat back Sebastien was watching her.
All the melancholy had gone and the playboy's
smile had returned. His glance went from her to
the statuette and back. The smile widened. He was
laughing at her.

Suddenly, her heart rate increased. Usually, she
could fight off that telltale hitch in her breathing,
the clatter of her heartbeat. She'd push it back, in
the way she'd taught herself to do, and any moments
of discomfort would start to pass. But this time it
wasn't working.

On the little finger of her right hand was her
signet ring. The ruby-and-gold ring had been pre-

sented to her on her eighteenth birthday, as it was with every Ellamaese heir. She spun it mechanically round and round her finger, but she caught Sebastien's sharp gaze watching the action. It was the very ring that had carved the scar on his jaw.

She covered the ring with her other hand.

She desperately searched the table in front of her.

Amongst the dregs of dinner sat her glass of white wine, another of champagne—both barely touched—a chilled bottle of sparkling water, damp with condensation, and beside it an unused goblet. She fiddled with them, taking her time until they were all neatly lined up. And her heart began to slow at last. But she needed some water and not the kind on their table.

She beckoned to their waiter. 'A still water, please. At room temperature. One ice cube. One slice of lime.'

As the waiter left to do her bidding, there was a soft snort from the man beside her.

'You have a problem with my drink order?' she said.

'That wasn't a drink order. It's something you'd take on a cleansing retreat.'

Forcing herself to do it, and appear calm and in control, she looked him up and down as if his proximity was distasteful. 'Perhaps I feel in need of cleansing.'

'Perhaps,' he said. 'However, at this moment, Your Majesty, you might be wiser to retreat.'

She sent him a glacial stare. 'A Toivonen never retreats.'

'Ma'am, neither does a von Frohburg. If it's a fight you want, which you seem to have been spoiling for all evening, you may have one. But I'll warn you. I play to win.'

Sofia, the elder Onzain sister, passed by their table, hand in hand with a partner, on the way to the dance floor. He watched them for a moment.

'Although, instead of fighting I suppose we could dance,' Sebastien mused.

'Dance with you?' Agnesse said a little unevenly, ruffled by the intense glitter in his eyes. 'Thank you, but I'd rather wrestle with a hungry bear.'

He tilted his head and studied her, green eyes alight with challenge.

'Role play? I could do that.' His voice lowered to a veritable purr. 'If that's what you want.'

Thank goodness for the dim light in here. She'd just gone pink to her ears. What a schoolgirl error to encourage such familiarities. Keert would have been disappointed in her.

'But it's just a dance,' Seb said, studying the crush of couples. 'And it will be expected of us. What do you say to getting it over with? Strip the plaster off in one swift move.'

Agnesse's chin lifted in defence. 'If it's going to be that distasteful to you, let's not.'

'No, that won't do.' In a surge of power he was on his feet. An unfurling of legs and a flexing of broad shoulders that sent a flurry of excitement through her. He stretched out a hand. 'Do me the honour, hmm?'

Interested eyes had turned their way. Cameras, too, no doubt. She wanted nothing controversial to appear in tomorrow's papers. At the very least she'd promised her mother. Reluctantly, she stood, gave him her hand, and allowed the prince to escort her to the dance floor.

Of course, he moved beautifully, expertly guiding her round the floor. It was so easy to follow his lead she even allowed herself to relax a little. Those moments of panic had passed and the challenging part of the evening was over.

'See,' he said, smiling down at her. 'This is perfectly pleasant.'

'I suppose you dance well enough.'

He inclined his head. 'Even if it feels like that compliment was grudgingly given, thank you.'

'I'm sure it's only because you've had so much opportunity to practise,' she added quickly.

There was no flippant response this time. Instead, his brow creased.

'Yes, there's been women. I like women and I'll make no apology for that.' He held her gaze, ramping up the heat in her belly. 'I might even like you. If you'd let me.'

She made a sound that she'd meant to be derisive but actually came out more of a whimper. She stared at the knot on his bow tie, helplessly wondering what he might do with a woman he liked.

'You're prickly but not that hard to like,' he said.

The scarlet gown of the comtesse danced into view. She was in the arms of a young diplomat who looked thoroughly entranced. How did women do that? Agnesse had no idea how to flirt, how to attract a man, and anyway, what would be the point when ultimately she was the Ice Queen and he would only be disappointed?

Sebastien followed the direction of her gaze.

'She's not what you think, you know. It amuses her to be seen as a femme fatale but much of the gossip is untrue. The comtesse uses her influence to raise millions for charities across Europe. She prefers not to make a big thing of it.'

Sofia passed by with her dance partner again. Agnesse felt a sharp stab of something like jealousy as Sebastien's gaze lingered briefly on the couple.

'You're saying that all the stories are false?'

He turned his attention back to her. He knew exactly which story she was referring to.

'Not entirely. But it wasn't a weekend. It was one night. And only *one* woman,' he said for emphasis. 'It meant nothing. For either of us. We were both bored and in need of entertainment.'

'You engage in the most intimate of acts out of boredom?' She could have bitten off her tongue. How prim had that sounded?

'Ma'am,' he purred, 'if you haven't derived pleasure from the intimate act, as you call it, I venture your lover hasn't been doing it right.'

Her lover was long gone and since that first and only time with him, she hadn't been doing it at all. But she wouldn't dare divulge that to this man. He'd probably see it as a challenge.

'But I did nothing to correct the story,' Sebastien continued. 'The d'Onzains are amused by their notoriety and the embellished story helped my cousin at the time. He'd just been jilted by his fiancée. It gave the press something more scandalous to salivate over.'

'Oh… I see.'

Sebastien's amused gaze settled back on her. 'Yes. I'm not the faithless creature you think I am.'

She wrestled with that surprising revelation for a moment. That he'd brought censure down on his own head to support his cousin.

'Difficult, isn't it? Admitting I'm not the complete scoundrel you thought.'

She tipped her chin upward. 'You still broke my sister's heart. She was only sixteen.'

His gaze narrowed sharply on her. 'And that fact alone should have told you I would have done nothing inappropriate. I was mindful of her youth. We'd met a month before at a friend's house. I remember we had a pleasant conversation but nothing more. Then at that wedding reception we all attended, she walked into a room, without preamble or invitation, where two adults were holding a private conversation. She behaved like an ill-mannered child and she was reprimanded as such.'

'You could have let her down gently.'

'There was no *letting down* to be done. All the interest had been on her side. I had done nothing to encourage it.'

The other dancers had all edged farther away, leaving a gap for the queen and the prince to dance unhindered. But Agnesse barely noticed.

'That's not her version of events.'

He stared down his nose at her. 'I'm not surprised she lied to you about what happened.'

'Or she isn't the one who lied.'

The hand at her waist tightened, then relaxed again.

'Look. I'm trying to be the gracious one here. Another man may try to get even for your very public slight that day.'

'Get even? I was defending Isobel. You were in the wrong. We are already even.'

'No.' He swirled her round. 'We are not.'

They danced in silence for a moment. She tried to ignore the impact of the strong, vital body close to hers and the realisation that she might have placed herself in the grip of a hungry bear, after all.

'I had no interest in your sister,' he said at last. 'Still don't. I am, however, finding myself drawn to *her* sister. Even if she is rather difficult.'

'I'm not difficult. I'm merely disinterested and

I assure you, I'm immune to whatever charms you think you have.'

'Is that so?'

Had she imagined it or had he just inched her closer? 'And what charms are those, hmm? The good looks? The wit?'

'The arrogance? The conceit?' she suggested, tartly.

He chuckled. 'I know you enjoyed watching me conduct the auction. I saw every emotion that crossed your face. You can't hide it. You like me.'

'You're deluded,' she said through her teeth, but her breasts tingled as they brushed his chest. She summoned a smile for a couple dancing by and fought to contain the growing feeling of giddy excitement at being in this man's arms.

'You didn't like the comtesse putting her hands on me.'

'Whatever happened at the dinner table was between—'

The corner of his mouth tilted. 'So you were watching me then, too? But I meant before that. When she approached us at the start of the evening. I thought you were about to leap between us.' He pulled her closer and rested his cheek against her temple. She felt the warm caress of his breath as he murmured, 'You've no need to be jealous, Your Majesty.'

How was he doing this? Making her feel so defenceless and unsteady and yet so thrillingly awake at the same time.

But this was the man who'd appeared so beguiling once before and then dismissed her as being unworthy of him. Her? A woman who took her role seriously and worked hard to earn the respect of her people. He may have forgotten that but she had not. Despite what she'd discovered about him tonight, wasn't he still essentially a man who used his royal title for nothing but his own gain, who enjoyed his status but assumed none of the responsibility that went with it?

She leant away so she could look directly into his eyes. 'You're quite mistaken. I wasn't at all jealous. You might have a handsome face but I have no interest in you. How could I? The second son of a second son who pursues pleasure and little else? You are not, nor ever could be, in my league.'

She felt the anger rip through him like a wildfire, consuming the softly teasing prince. In its place it left a man whose charming expression had become a cold mask.

She hadn't meant to insult him so badly and regretted it at once. But she was struggling to cope with his charm offensive and her body's wayward reactions to the closeness of his.

She was completely unprepared for what he did next.

He shifted his grip, tipped her backwards in his arms, and before she could stop him, fastened his mouth over hers. Too shocked to respond, she let him kiss her. His lips and his tongue taking shocking liberties.

He tasted of things she could hardly name but wanted more of.

It's passion, she thought dimly. Wrapped in a masculine feast of soft lips, and an enticing body that was hard and hot. She would've been breathless if she could breathe at all.

It had never felt like this with Eerik. Not even for a moment. This need to be closer still, to mould their bodies together. She slid her hand from his shoulder to curl about his neck. She arched her hips to press closer to his, revelling in the feeling of being weightless, of being held so securely in his arms.

Then suddenly his mouth, and all that tempting softness, was gone. Her eyes fluttered open, her gaze refocused to clash with his, oddly dark and forbidding.

'Now I think we are even,' he said.

And in a move, so swift she hardly felt it happening, she was upright, back on her own two feet, and he was striding away.

Leaving her marooned amongst the cream of European society who, stripped of their elegant manners by the sight, gawked at her like fishwives at a street brawl.

CHAPTER FOUR

IT WAS TEN minutes in his limo across Vienna, then a farther five, striding across foyers and into lifts, before Seb reached the sanctuary of his hotel suite, where his simmering temper drove him straight to the bar. He dumped a generous measure of whisky into a tumbler and knocked it back, grimacing at the burn as it went down. The label identified it as a very fine thirty-year-old single malt, but Seb tasted nothing. Nothing but her seared onto his lips.

He should never have kissed her.

He tore his bow tie loose, flung his tux jacket onto the nearest sofa, then refilled the glass.

Why the hell had he kissed her?

Because she'd offended him, dismissed him in the worst possible way. Agnesse of Ellamaa had crossed a line by insulting him again. *Second son*: the moniker that had tainted his entire life. This time she'd actually dared say it to his face.

But his instinctive retaliation had seriously back-fired when he'd tasted all that honeyed sweetness, when he'd felt her melt in his arms.

She was a beauty, yes, but there was more. Was it because she was firmly off-limits? Because he had no intention of getting entangled with her. That kiss was the end of it. He never let a woman trouble him in this way. Especially not a royal one. He pre-

ferred to give any kind of royalty a wide berth. He'd
had his fill of its pettiness and politicking that sur-
rounded his family. He wanted as little as possible
to do with that life. He'd have renounced his own
title but the von Frohburgs would love that, and he
wouldn't give them the satisfaction.

And he owed Leo. The best of them by far and
the only one he considered family, who'd been in
his corner for as long as Seb could remember. More
of a brother than Max, his actual elder brother,
would ever be. Seb kept his title and his link to the
von Frohburgs to support Leo.

And for his mother.

The young woman of humble birth who, despite
what the von Frohburgs believed, had married a
prince for love and nothing more.

He had a handful of photos of her. In all of them
she was simply dressed, wearing a wedding band
only. Obviously no interest in the trappings of her
husband's wealth and status. She'd never even allowed them to call her *princess*, though royal ob-
servers noted she'd behaved with all the dignity
of one.

Fabienne Bonfils had wanted Prince Georg the
man, and not his title. But Seb would keep his, in honour and remembrance of her. And to spite his pompous relatives who hated the fact it was his by right.

Did Agnesse share their prejudice? Was that why
she'd taunted him?

'We are already even,' she'd told him, lifting her

chin in challenge. But the light had glowed on the lustrous pearls of her earrings, and the luminous perfection of her skin, and for that moment all he wanted was to discover if that place just beneath her jaw was as tender as it looked, and would she moan for him if he pressed his lips there?

She'd been wearing pearl earrings the very first time he'd set eyes on her. Tiny pearl studs and a delicate gold necklace, with a pendant in the shape of an 'A'. He remembered she'd tied her hair back with a blue scarf, the same colour as her eyes. Seb had been in the audience at her school prize giving.

From time to time and for appearances' sake, his father behaved as if he actually cared about his younger son, which was why Seb had been with him that day. Prince Georg presenting prizes to youngsters while enthusing over their achievements would be more credible if he had one of his own children in tow.

Seb had winked at her as she waited anxiously to give her speech. In the reception afterwards she stood talking to other guests. Bathed in a pool of sunshine that transformed her blond hair into a golden halo, he was convinced he was looking at an angel. Then she looked up, their eyes had met, and she smiled at him. In all his life he'd never seen anything more enchanting.

But his father had seen the direction of his gaze and later, as they'd descended the stairs to the exit where their car waited, he'd chastised him. 'Take your thoughts off the Toivonen girl. She's heir to a throne and not for the likes of you.'

He'd snapped back. Hiding his hurt at yet another of his father's slights by dismissing the girl. Something about her pretty face, but that intellectually she was not his equal and so of no interest.

It was almost word for word what Agnesse had flung at him tonight.

Seb slugged back more whisky.

She'd heard him that day.

The smart of his father's dismissal had made him lash out, belittling the girl without a thought to ease his own hurt, never imagining she would overhear.

His fingers went to the scar on his jaw where her ring had gouged a sliver of skin. Was that what the punch had been about? The excuse about Isobel hiding the real hurt Agnesse had felt?

Well, he'd never have to see the Queen of Ellamaa again, or suffer any more of her insults and jibes. Nor wonder how it would be to bed the woman who'd melted so thoroughly in his arms.

Ellamaa. It had the sound of a magical kingdom. Where a man might find himself enchanted by its Fairy Queen. Or, more likely, frozen to death by one of her glacial stares.

But as he'd just discovered—or perhaps known all along—Ellamaa's queen wasn't cold. Beneath all that icy reserve the woman burned hot. The sweet temptation of her response had made it hard to set her away from him back in the ballroom.

She was a warm, sensual creature. He'd seen the seeds of it that day at the prize giving. When she'd smiled at him and he'd been unable to stop himself smiling back.

But a few years after that not only had she punched him, she'd also belittled him, and today she'd repeated that he was beneath her.

She'd got off lightly. A kiss—it had just been a kiss—to prove he wasn't as repellent and beneath her as she'd claimed.

Seb shoved a hand through his hair. Even so, it had not been the act of a gentleman to try and prove that so publicly. He certainly shouldn't have abandoned her on the dance floor. He took another slug of whisky.

Why did the one woman in the world who could practically scramble his DNA have to be so difficult you needed a black belt in ducking and diving just to hold a conversation?

Voices raised in the corridor outside interrupted his musings.

His suite shared the top floor of the hotel with only one other. He'd dressed for the evening on his private jet and gone straight to the gala from the airport so there'd been no chance of bumping into its occupant in the hotel corridors.

Though of course, Seb knew exactly who it was.

Your Majesty. Please open the door.

Ma'am, you must let me back in.

Yes, Agness of Ellamaa was just across the hallway and still causing trouble by the sounds of it.

The voices were getting louder and more agitated. Seb tried to tune it out. It was nothing to do with him. Let her team see to her.

But now the pounding of a fist and a more determined female voice. 'Ma'am? Agnesse? Open the door.'

That they'd resorted to her given name was an indication of their concern. It got him to his feet and out into the corridor.

Gathered outside the queen's door was her security team, a small, agitated woman whom he presumed was a maid, and the hotel butler assigned to the Royal Suite.

'What's going on?'

The maid rushed towards him.

'Oh, sir. The queen asked me to get Christina for her and then she locked me out. She's never done anything like this before. I don't know what's come over her.'

'Maybe she wants some peace and quiet after an evening doing her duty.' He sent them a pointed look but they didn't appear to get the irony.

But her maid's alarm was genuine and worrying. Seb felt a prick of conscience. After what he'd done, he should at least reassure himself there was nothing seriously wrong.

'What about the staff entrance?'

The butler looked uncomfortable. 'That key card isn't working. I've sent for another.'

On cue the hotel manager arrived. Apologising

to Seb while simultaneously scolding the butler for the grievous sin of inconveniencing His Highness. Seb doubted it was the man's fault and said so, gaining a grateful smile for his pains.

Seb took the key card from the manager, opening the door himself and ordering everyone to wait outside, reassuring them he'd summon them if they were needed. Agnesse had kicked her staff out for a reason. Whatever was happening she didn't want them to witness it. He could identify with that. Hadn't there been times when he felt the same?

He began searching the suite, calling for her. The sitting room was empty. The door to the private terrace stood open, but the elegant space, with its magnificent views of the city and its planters of roses and cherry trees, was deserted. So, too, was the bedroom, though someone had been there because the covers were awry as if desperate hands had tried to drag them off. Then Seb heard a noise coming from the bathroom. He headed for the door. Pushed it wide.

And there she was, crumpled in a heap on the tiled floor: bundled in a white robe, hair an untidy mass of gold, and face scraped free of makeup. His glorious nemesis.

In the midst of the mother of all panic attacks.

There'd barely been time to fabricate a reason to get Dorel out of her suite, to lock her door, and stagger back to the bed, before the nausea and dizziness overtook her. She'd somehow got to the bathroom, wanting to splash cold water on her face. But once there her legs had buckled beneath her and she'd slumped to the floor.

As the room spun and the pain in her chest got worse, she heard the hammering on her door, her team yelling her name. She regretted alarming them, but she couldn't let anyone see her like this. However bad it got. They mustn't know she had these moments. No one must know.

But now a new voice called to her, calmer and closer, from inside the suite itself. She recognised it instantly.

Not him. Anyone but him to see her this way.

But even as that thought arrived, another came quickly on its heels.

You'll be safe with him. You don't have to be alone this time.

Inexplicable though it was, after he'd humiliated her so publicly, when the prince's tall figure appeared in the doorway, she reached for him.

'Seb…astien.'

In a few long strides he was there, dropping to his haunches before her, taking both her hands in his. Searching her face, his expression all concern.

'Heart…pounding. Scared,' she told him on a series of gasping breaths.

'Agnesse,' he said, gently. 'I know this is frightening but what you're experiencing is a panic attack. You'll get through it, I promise you, and I'll be here to help you until you do.'

He was so wrong. It wasn't an attack. This was worse than anything she'd experienced before. She'd had episodes like these where her heart had raced, her breath coming in short, choppy bursts, but those times she'd managed to control them. This time she couldn't because surely she was dying. Her heart was beating hard enough to burst out of her chest.

'Look at me.' The command was gentle but a command all the same. He waited until her eyes fixed on his. 'We're going to breathe together. Breathe in, Agnesse.'

He was so calm and steady. How could he be when she was on her bathroom floor? *Dying.*

'Breathe,' he repeated, squeezing her hands.

She tried. Nothing happened. She couldn't do it. She was never going to breathe properly again.

'It's all right. I know you're frightened but it will be okay if you try and follow what I do.' He inhaled through his nose and blew out a long, slow breath from his mouth.

She copied him. Sort of. The iron fist clamped about her lungs loosened enough for her to drag in some air.

'Good girl. Now out.'

She pushed the air out, still feeling like she might suffocate. But Sebastien continued breathing in and out slowly himself, counting for her. 'In two three. Now out two three.' She tried to copy him while clutching his hands. They felt so solid, like her lifeline.

But she was doing it. Her shallow, gasping breaths were getting deeper.

'Now, tell me five things you can see,' he said.

What? She had to breathe first. Surely, that was her priority.

'How…how—'

'I've seen this before,' he said, answering the question she couldn't frame. 'At a mental health charity I work with. Now, five things, Agnesse.'

She struggled to process that. Not supported. Worked *with*. The playboy helping out at a charity? That astonishing thought shocked her enough that she answered his question.

'You,' she said.

His mouth quirked. 'That's one. What else?'

The room was still spinning but she did her best to look around.

'A gold tap.'

'Good. And?'

'Two—two gold taps?'

He smiled in earnest now. 'Nice try. But I'm still waiting for a third thing.'

'So—so picky,' she said, shivering now. 'Okay. M—mirror. Marble b—bath.' Her heart was slowing at last. 'And t—towel,' she said.

'Good girl. Now four things you can hear.'

Who put him in charge? 'Someone b—being a p—pain?'

He chuckled. 'You'll thank me later. What next?'

'My—my teeth chattering.'

'Yeah, what a racket. I can hardly hear myself think.' He reached forward to gently push her hair back from her face. 'Number three?'

'Air con.'

She'd said that without a stumble.

The wall behind her separated this suite from the corridor outside, where she could hear Dorel babbling and Christina doing her best to calm her.

'And my maid, having a fit.'

'I don't blame her. You've given us a fright.'

'Sorry.'

She breathed out. Slower, easier. That terrifying tightness in her chest was easing. His beautiful face became serious. And kind.

'You lost your papa and became queen in the same moment. You're grieving and grappling with your new role all at the same time. I'm not surprised you're having moments like these.'

She gazed up at him, forgetting to be guarded, drinking him in. This wasn't the man she'd expected after the evening's exchanges.

'Do you think you can stand?' he asked.

Her legs were jelly. A wave of exhaustion was sapping all her strength. Standing wouldn't be happening anytime soon.

'Give me a moment. I'll be okay soon. You can go now if you like.'

He looked appalled at that suggestion. 'Not likely.

I'm staying until I know you're okay. Would you like me to call a doctor?'

'No!'

He raised a brow.

'I mean, no thank you, because what could a doctor do? I'll be fine shortly and then I have work to get on with.'

'You've just spent several hours working at that gala. It's time to rest.'

'But I still have a report to read and emails to answer tonight.'

He rolled his eyes at her. 'How is that self-care, hmm? Don't you know anything about coping with panic attacks?'

Actually, no, because she'd never had one this bad before.

'I'll be fine. Honestly.' She tried to reassure him.

'Stubborn woman,' he said, suddenly scooping her up. 'You're not working again tonight if I have anything to do with it.' He carried her from the bathroom and even if she'd had the strength to protest, right then she didn't want to because in his strong arms, she felt safer and less alone than she had in months.

It felt so good to hold her, but hell, he shouldn't be revelling in it. She'd just suffered a panic attack. Lighten the mood, he thought. *Now.*

'God, you're a weight.'

The woman in his arms mumbled something.

'Excuse me?'

'I said the correct address would be, "You're a weight, Your Majesty."'

He made a derisive snort. 'Seems to me it's all the royal stuff that's got you into this state, so let's dispense with titles, shall we? Tonight I'm just Seb.'

'Okay… Seb,' she murmured, and sweet pleasure flared in his chest at the sound of his name on her lips. He set her on her feet beside the bed, careful to keep one hand on her arm in case she swayed. With the other he gave a little tug on the collar of her bathrobe.

'On or off?'

There, that was suitably avuncular. Not a hint of anything suggestive to it. Which was essential. Because everything else about this situation was screaming danger. He left her pulling at the belt of her robe while he focused on setting the bed to rights.

He could do this. He could help her and then walk away. There'd be no repeat of what happened on the dance floor and he'd give no hint, by even so much as a sideways glance, of what she was doing to his self-control.

Then he saw what she was wearing beneath her robe. Not a silky wisp of a chemise, which he'd expected—and braced himself for. Nor something helpfully chaste, falling from neck to ankle in virginal white cotton.

No, the nightwear preferences for the Queen of Ellamaa went in an entirely different direction.

The all-encompassing bathrobe had fallen away to reveal a fine linen cami with shoestring straps and ruffled hem, plus shorts edged with tiny matching frills, the whole outfit strewn with daisy motifs. The ensemble was not only rather adorable but also showing way too much leg for his comfort. The shorts had even ridden up on one side to offer a glimpse of shapely buttock. Seb dropped his gaze and redoubled his efforts at straightening the crisp cotton sheets and silken eiderdown.

When he'd finished Agnesse slumped to the bed, oblivious to the effect she was having on him. 'I wish I was home,' she said.

So did he. Hundreds of miles away in gloomy Grimentz Castle. Far removed from this sumptuous hotel bedroom, with its plump pillows, soft lighting, and half-naked beauty.

Over the sudden hoarseness in his throat he said, 'Ellamaa?'

'Not just Ellamaa. In the Summer Palace. It's ten miles outside the city but it could be a hundred. It's so peaceful. It's the one place I can really relax.'

She looked up at him again, with big, haunted eyes and he knew he should turn on his heel and get the hell out of there, before he did something reckless.

'I realise I've been difficult this evening and it's a lot to ask, but…would you hold me again?'

Something exactly like that for instance.

Bad, *bad* idea.

The lustful beast in him clamoured to do it, to get acquainted with all the luscious curves and hollows on show. But in the mental tussle that followed—take shameless advantage of an emotionally vulnerable woman or do the right thing—the gentleman prince won out.

Just.

'That wouldn't be appropriate,' he said.

'Please. Only for a moment.' Her luminous gaze fixed hopefully on him.

'Why don't I fetch your maid?' he suggested.

'Dorel will fuss and worry and ask lots of questions and I can't face that right now. Surely, you know how it is? Don't you have moments when you wished they would just leave you alone?'

Damn it.

He ran a hand through his hair, knowing she had him because, yes, he'd had times like that. Days when he wanted to hide from everyone. But always a servant stood nearby or security hovered on the other side of a door.

So he lifted the bed covers and helped her climb in, and while she snuggled down he heeled off his shoes, placed his watch on the nightstand then lay down beside her. Instantly, she flowed into his arms, tucking her head beneath his chin. Like she belonged there.

Her perfume enveloped him. An elegant classic that was familiar, but which he'd never found quite so appealing before. Seb cleared his throat.

'How many times have you experienced an attack?' That was good. Get on to something practical, something that would distract him from the heady scent, the supple limbs, and enticing curves of the woman in his arms.

'Five. Always at night. But this has been the worst.' Her fingers toyed with the edge of his collar. 'I hate how helpless I feel. Being so out of control.'

He remembered the glasses lined up at the banquet. 'And you like to be in control of everything?'

'Don't you?'

His life had been troubled much less by the protocols that governed hers. He'd taken a grim satisfaction in flouting the ones that had. Less so now his cousin was monarch, but he didn't relish control. It smacked too much of his father's regimented world.

'I prefer spontaneity,' he said. 'It's good for the soul to let things just happen every now and then.'

'I can't indulge in that. I have too much work to do.' She adjusted her position, and her thighs brushed against his.

'But surely even a queen is allowed days off,' he said through suddenly gritted teeth.

'I can't afford to. Not everyone agreed with the changes to the succession and I know some of them are waiting for me to fail. I can't give them any excuse to doubt me. Papa started the monarchy on a new path but we discussed the ways we can help our people even more. I have to make those things happen.'

Seb heard the determination in that statement. But also the fear that not all her countrymen supported her and shared her vision. What allies did this young queen have?

He tightened his embrace.

'How have you managed your attacks in the past?'

'I haven't,' she said with a bitter laugh. 'I just hid in my rooms until they were over. I've never told anyone about them.'

'Not even your doctor?'

Her hair tickled his chin as she shook her head.

Even though tonight she'd been confrontational and he bore a scar as a perpetual reminder of this woman's temper, the thought of her dealing with her attacks all alone crushed something inside him.

'Tonight you don't have to get through it alone. You have me to help,' he said, giving her back a reassuring rub, and for his pains discovering the delicate ridge of her spine.

She made a soft sound, like a sigh of relief. 'When I was a girl, if I was upset or worried, Papa would distract me by telling a story. It always made me feel better.' She nestled closer. 'Perhaps you could do that?'

Seriously? This was a first. In bed with a barely dressed woman and all the entertainment she wanted from him was stories?

'Er...that's not my forte.'

She tilted her head to look up at him. 'You told all sorts of tales when you ran the auction tonight.'

'Hardly the same thing.'

'Please.' She pressed a palm over his sternum in supplication.

Why, *why* hadn't he stayed in his own rooms? Left her team to sort this out.

She was silent. Waiting...

Okay, he'd got himself into this and if, to extricate himself again, he had to be Seb the storyteller, so be it.

'Once upon a time there was a beautiful queen,' he began, 'who was brave and strong but thought she had to slay every dragon single-handed.'

Agnesse's soft huff of breath feathered through his shirt, warming flesh and bone. Right over his heart.

Seb swallowed hard, then said, 'But when it got too bad she put on her favourite nightwear, the one strewn with magical daisies, and remembered all the faith her beloved papa had in her.'

Her face was hidden, but he knew for a certainty she'd just smiled at that.

'Daisies were his favourite flowers,' she said.

'Because he knew they contained magic. Magic that would help a clever princess become a great queen.'

Her fingers made a little fist in his shirt front. 'I don't feel like a great queen. I feel like I'm never quite good enough. I badly want to make Papa proud. But it's been hard. I miss him so much, Seb.'

His name again. And said in such a small, faraway voice. Compassion for this grieving woman made him kiss the top of her head, then turn his cheek against her hair. 'Trust me, he would be very proud of you.'

Her fingers crept higher, slipping inside his shirt to caress the hollow at the base of his throat.

'What did you mean earlier, about not everyone being blessed by kindly fathers?' she asked quietly.

He'd regretted revealing that much about himself and he'd hated the flash of pity he'd seen in her expression when he had.

When he didn't answer she lifted her head to look him in the eye. 'Seb, was your father unkind?'

And damn it, there was the pity again. But something else, too. A compassion that warmed him—and, surprisingly, loosened his tongue.

'Mostly he was indifferent. But occasionally, yes, he was unkind.'

An understatement.

'Why was he unkind?' Her soft voice was full of disbelief.

Why indeed? The question Seb had asked himself for much of his thirty-two years. He'd stopped when he'd decided the only man who could truly answer it was already gone. Or perhaps because he knew the answer anyway: it was because Seb had survived.

'On my fourth birthday my father announced to me that he wished I'd never been born.'

Agnesse gasped and slid an arm around his waist. 'I'm so sorry. Do you want to talk about it?'

Seb's earliest memory was from that night. When his father had burst into his room. Roaring drunk and savage with it.

I lost her because of you, you little monster, he'd spat, spraying spittle everywhere. *You killed her. It's your fault. I wish you had died instead.*

Then two footmen had rushed in with Leo's father, who'd yelled at his brother to pull himself together and slapped him hard across the face. Prince Georg had broken down, sobbing uncontrollably as they dragged him from the room. A nanny was sent to settle Seb again, but once she had gone, he'd crept from his bed and slept under it all night and for a whole month after, in case his father came back.

He'd never told anyone, not even Leo, about that night. No one else ever spoke of it. Certainly, his father had never apologised, never took back what he'd said to his young son. While Seb had tried to bury that memory, the agony of it had never truly gone away. His only surviving parent hadn't wanted him. His father had been dead for seven years but all that bitter, blighting hurt still resurfaced now.

Agnesse had turned her cheek to his chest and pressed her body against the length of his. He could easily lose himself in the comfort of that. So easily. But he couldn't allow that to happen.

'That's a story for another day,' he said, shifting his weight, releasing her from his arms instead. 'And now you're feeling better perhaps it would be best if I go. Your team will be worrying.'

Better to go, yes, but not what his body demanded when she looked at him with soft, unguarded eyes, or trailed burning fingertips over his skin. Not when he felt the press of her breasts against him and the tantalising heat of her body next to his.

'They'll know you'd have called them if they were needed. Stay,' she said, lifting a hand to his jaw. 'Just a bit longer. Please.'

A fingertip found his scar. 'I'm sorry about this,' she said, stroking it gently, then shocked him by pressing her lips to it. She leant back and looked up at him with a bashful smile.

'There, I've kissed it better.'

It was the briefest of touches, but it sent his heart clattering around in his chest.

Now her gaze darkened and dropped to his mouth. 'Will you kiss me again? Like you did on the dance floor.'

Oh, God, yes.

'No. That would be a very bad idea.'

'You did it before.'

'And I shouldn't have.'

'But you wanted to get even.'

He released a strand of hair caught in her eye-lashes. 'In the moment, yes. But now I apologise. That was not the act of a gentleman.'

'What if I want you to this time?'

'No,' he said firmly, as much for his benefit as hers. They were not going there.

'It's one kiss. One little kiss. How could that hurt?'

Lord, she knew *nothing*.

Her face fell. 'Is it because I'm not good enough? The famous playboy is in bed with me and he won't even kiss me. Do I lack something all your other women had?' Her eyes sparked with anger. 'You took Sofia d'Onzain to bed just because you were bored. Yet, you won't kiss me at all. She must be so much more attractive than I am,' she snapped, flinging herself from the bed and stomping to the bathroom.

Seb collapsed backwards onto the covers and stared at the ceiling. He *definitely* should have stayed in his own suite. First, she hated his guts; now she wanted kisses.

Give him strength.

He exhaled heavily, climbed from the bed, and crossed to the closed door of the bathroom.

'It's not that I don't want to,' he said, raising his voice to be heard through the heavy wood and the sound of a tap running.

The water stopped. 'Then why won't you kiss me? You were happy enough to do it when there was an audience.' The door flew open. 'Is *that* the problem? You need someone to see. Shall I call in my maid? Our security? Give them a show.'

'Agnesse,' he warned.

'Oh, don't bother.' She shoved past him and headed back to bed. 'Don't worry, your virtue is safe with me. I'm the Ice Queen, remember. No man in his right mind would want to touch me.'

He heard the hurt; how could he not? He'd have to be made of ice himself to have missed it, and despite everything his chest clenched. He padded back to the bed, sank down beside her. She'd curled up under the covers, with her back to him. A small, blonde-haired ball of misery.

'You're an attractive woman. Who wouldn't want to kiss you? But surely, you can see it would be crazy for us to give in to the impulse. Especially in here. Alone.'

'Afraid you won't be able to control yourself?' The snide comeback was muffled by her pillow.

'Yes, actually. That's precisely what scares me.'

She turned her head to peek up at him. 'So you do find me attractive.'

'Yes. But I already told you that. Now it looks like you're fishing for compliments. And that's *not* an attractive quality.'

But Agnesse was grinning, then looking coy, and now, Heaven help him, she'd shuffled closer. Her hands were on his chest and she gazed up at him through her lashes. 'So kiss me. Just once. To show me you mean it.'

Her hand slid up to his neck and pulled his face down towards her. 'Look, I'll even make it easier for you.' She closed her eyes and puckered up.

The last time he'd had sex with a woman she'd been wearing expensive, barely there black lace underwear. She'd draped herself over the bed in a practised pose.

Yet, this woman, dressed in daisy-strewn shorts with her eyes squeezed shut, sent lust screaming through him.

'I really am trying to be the gentleman here,' he said, his voice gruff. Maybe he was attempting to convince himself even more than her.

Her fingers slid upward, to curl around his neck and caress the hair at the back of his head. A ripple of awareness tingled over his scalp.

'I don't want the gentleman. I want the playboy.' There was a thread of vulnerability in her voice now. Like a plea, not to be rejected again. Seb remembered that bastard of a fiancé, the things he'd implied about her. Cold. Unresponsive. That wasn't the woman he'd kissed on the dance floor or who gazed up at him now.

Okay.

One kiss.

Surely, he could handle that?

He wanted those shadows gone from her beautiful blue eyes. He wanted that hurt gone from her lovely face altogether. He let her bring their faces closer. Their mouths to meet. There it was again, the jolt of energy that shook him. Need and desire surged to life. But he'd control it.

It would just be a kiss.

Seb slid his hands into her hair, fingers gently cupping her skull so he could hold her closer and increase the pressure of their mouths. She tasted of everything a man could want, like sunshine and happiness and wild, untrammelled passion. He followed eagerly when she rolled onto her back and pulled him down on top of her.

A few moments more, then he'd stop.

Her hands slid down his back, her fingers tugging his shirt loose from his trousers, and then there was the hot glide of them over his naked back.

Seb groaned. Shifted his position so he was stretched out over her. But he couldn't touch anything. There were bedclothes and an adorable daisy-covered sleep set in his way. And, boy, did he want to touch.

With an open mouth she kissed him again, sliding her tongue to tangle with his. There was more enthusiasm than skill, but the impact rocketed through him all the same. He was getting lost, losing his grip, losing control. Phrases he'd never used in connection with a woman. He always remained emotionally detached. Always. It was a matter of self-preservation.

Could he do it? Make love to Agnesse and not get

involved? The woman who'd haunted his dreams since the moment he set eyes on her. Who'd been the fantasy creature he'd measured every lover against since that day. Wanting her memory to be eclipsed by another and yet never finding a woman who had.

And the fantasy was nothing compared to the living, breathing woman writhing beneath him, tugging urgently at his clothes. Her hands were trying to push his trousers down his hips; when they couldn't they dipped beneath the waistband of his trousers, caressing the small of his back, then lower to the rise of his buttocks. He groaned and ground his hips against her.

He stopped fighting it. He wasn't strong enough, after all. He rose up, dragged his shirt over his shoulders, and flung it on the floor, tore the sheets and duvet out of his way. Then he was back on her, his hands beneath the hem of that tantalising, whisper-thin cami, pushing it higher, exposing her breasts to his hungry gaze—and mouth. When he laved them with his tongue, she cried out, shoving her hands into his hair to keep his head where it was. When he took one rosy, puckered nipple between his teeth her hips arched up off the bed.

'Seb,' she panted. 'Oh, Seb.'

He'd never heard anything more profoundly arousing than that soft plea. For a plea it was. To take her higher, to show her more. And he would, all in good time. But she was wriggling, frantically trying to get out of her shorts, and they'd snagged halfway down her hips. His shirt was off. Her night-wear all but gone. His erection strained painfully against his fly.

'Slow down,' he groaned, as much to himself as to her. This was going way too fast. And not fast enough. He wanted to be inside her with a fervour he'd never known. Her body was perfection, as if some celestial creature had read his mind and cre-ated a woman just for him. The feel of her skin, the way her breasts filled his palms, the flare of her hips, voluptuous and fertile.

Fertile?

That pulled him up short.

'Wait,' he said. 'Are you protected?'

She gazed up at him, uncomprehending. Devour-ing him with those stunning blue eyes, but saying nothing.

He took that as a no.

He had protection in his own suite but going back for it was out of the question. The beast inside him howled in frustration, but this was stopping now. However much he wanted her he would never, *ever* risk getting a woman pregnant.

Although…

He mightn't be prepared, but this grand hotel surely would be.

In the bathroom his faith was rewarded. Amidst the high-end toiletries and designer perfumes, was a discreet but generous stash of condoms.

Seb grabbed a handful in his size, sent up a prayer of thanks to the gods of housekeeping and headed back to the bedroom.

Several condom packets landed on the nightstand. Agnesse was a little daunted by the number. How many times did he expect to do this? Seb stripped off the rest of his clothes then knelt between her splayed thighs, ripping open a packet with his teeth and rolling the condom over his erection.

She watched; how could she not? A naked Seb was a sight to behold.

He lowered himself down, supported on one elbow. But in those moments, when he'd left her to search the bathroom, reality had intruded and she'd become acutely aware that in her urgency to get naked with him, and finally banish her lingering fear that she was frigid, she'd been inexpertly dragging off her own clothes. How gauche. She hid her dismay in the pillow.

A hand slid to the nape of her neck. 'Look at me, Agnesse,' he said, gently. And she did, though not where he meant. She sneaked a glance down to the jut of his erection—and gulped.

It was thick and long. How was that ever going to fit?

'*Chérie*, you've done this before, *oui*?'

That lapse into French, with its tender endearment, stole around her heart like the caress of warm fingers.

She gazed up into eyes turned black with desire. A little of her failing confidence flowed back.

'Not for a while and even then, it was only once.' She was embarrassed at how little experience she'd had compared to Seb. Would she be disappointing, put her limbs in the wrong place, not know where to touch, not please him at all? Would it be just another bout of sex to him?

'If you want to stop, *chérie*, we stop. We only go as far as you want.'

But the thing was she didn't want to stop. She wanted him to touch her, to kiss her breasts again, and feel sweet pleasure arrow straight to that place between her thighs. And she wanted to touch him, to run her tongue along the vein that bulged in sharp relief on his biceps, to put her mouth to that ridge of muscle low on his abdomen. Perhaps even lower, if she had the courage.

She reached up to cup his jaw, and her confidence soared when he closed his eyes and turned his head to press his lips into her palm. Maybe he did that with his other women, but she didn't care. Tonight he was with her.

'No, I don't want to stop.'

'As long as you are sure?'

She nodded.

But as he eased into her she gasped; it was too tight, too much. She struggled against him. But then his mouth was at her cheek, breathing soft words of encouragement. A litany of delight, matched by the caress of hands as one slid along her inner thigh, hooked beneath her knee and opened her wider for him. When he pushed in next time it was easier.

And it felt good.

He pulled back, and she felt him brace and this time sink deeper.

She felt so full of him, almost overwhelmed by the sensation. But she wanted this. She wanted to get lost in him and leave nothing of the old Agnesse behind. Tonight she would finally say goodbye to the Ice Queen.

She wanted something else, too; she wanted to see him come undone. This man, who'd been a lover to so many other women. She wanted a piece of him that was just hers and would only ever be hers. A sliver of emotion, of his *heart*; something of his that she would hold forever, even after this night together had become a distant memory.

Her first and only time had been with Eerik, and it had been painful. But that was so long ago, did it even count anymore? Nothing she'd felt then could compare with the glide of Seb's body inside hers.

Something within her that had been closed off and wound tight was unfurling. Because of him.

This.

This felt like her first time.

She forgot he'd ever been her enemy. As his hands caressed her, cupped her breasts, sent her pleasure soaring, she wondered if that man had ever really existed. His breathing was shallower, harsher; sweat glistened over his body. He was moving faster, thrusting harder. But she was with him, matching every groan, every sigh, every devouring kiss.

Until his hand slipped between them and his thumb slid right to where she was wet and hot.

Her breath stuttered in her throat. He rolled his hips and thumb with the same relentless rhythm, and now she was gasping and writhing and crying out. Incoherent, abandoned.

Triumphant.

Agnesse, the Ice Queen of Ellamaa, buried her face in her lover's neck and gave herself up to glorious, transcendental passion at last.

CHAPTER FIVE

THE GLIDE OF a palm along her flank roused Agnesse from her sleep. She cracked open an eye.

Oh now, there was a sight to wake up to. Propped up on one arm and gazing down on her was a tousled sex god, sporting a gorgeous lopsided smile.

'You're looking very pleased with yourself,' she said.

'I've just made love with a warm, giving beauty.' He took her mouth in a soft kiss. 'Why wouldn't I be pleased?'

She trailed her fingers along his jaw, fascinated by the scratch of early-morning stubble. 'Made love?' she repeated, dreamily.

The shutters came down at once.

'It's a figure of speech, Agnesse. Call it plain sex if you want. A coarser term would fit, too.' He captured those caressing fingers and pressed a perfunctory kiss to them. 'But I think that would jar in this beautiful room.'

Not love, then, or anything close to it, and he was keen she knew it. But there was nothing plain or coarse about what they'd done together. It was a revelation more like. Her body had responded in ways she'd never imagined it could. Already it was hungry for more. A throb of need beat low in her pelvis.

But he was untangling their limbs, throwing aside the sheets. 'It would be better if I weren't seen leaving your suite, and there'd be much less chance of that if I go now.'

She forced herself not to cling. Not to ask if they could meet up again.

What for, Agnesse? More casual sex? That was all there was on offer and however tempting that might be, what would be the point? Seb was not the man to give her what she really needed. A reliable prince consort for her country. A steadfast man to support her.

However, there was no reason to deny herself the pleasure of ogling as a stark-naked Seb walked about the room, gathering up his clothes. She rolled onto her stomach, propped her chin on her hands, and watched him. The spectacle of him taking *off* his clothes would be better, but this came a close second. She'd had no idea it could be so engrossing. He was tanned all over except for the paler skin of his buttocks. They disappeared from view as he stepped into tight black jersey boxers. But the fabric clung lovingly to every taut muscle so her gaze lingered there, until they, too, were covered by beautifully tailored trousers. Agnesse bit her lip as the zipper went up, recalling the pleasure she'd received when that zipper had come down. She mourned the loss of his bare torso but there was something enthralling about the flex of muscle and sinew as a man shrugged into his shirt.

He came back to her, smiling slightly at her rapt attention. He collected his watch from the night-stand.

'Thank you. Last night turned out much better than I'd anticipated.'

Her brows shot up. 'If rescuing me from my bath-room floor was better than you imagined, you must have had really low expectations.'

His expression tightened with concern then warmed again as it dropped to her breasts, plumped up between her and the mattress. 'But how much more delightful did our evening become after that?'

She fluttered her eyelashes at him and he chuck-led as he bent to drop a parting kiss to her brow.

She was okay with him leaving like this. Re-ally, she was.

She would revel in the discovery that Agnesse, the frigid queen, was not so cold, after all, and not let Seb's departure spoil the moment.

Only once he'd gone she felt the keenest disap-pointment, as if some vital element of her peace of mind had just walked out the door with him.

The stroll back into his suite was short, unevent-ful, and more importantly, unobserved. Other than by the respective security teams who were paid well for their discretion. Walking away and leaving Agnesse, all warm and willing, in bed had been the harder act to accomplish. Her blond hair tumbling about her shoulders, the plushness of her breasts, and her absolute focus as she watched him dress, nearly had him stripping off again and climbing back into bed beside her. He didn't do it because what if he'd slept again afterwards?

Slept? That had been a first. He'd never actually *slept* with a woman. It could lead to them getting the wrong idea. So he'd always left.

Until he hadn't.

Agnesse Toivonen was no Ice Queen but a woman of warmth and passion and curves—Lord, *those curves*. She was vulnerable, too, though she tried to hide it, and even as he told himself there would be nothing further between them, something warm and tender settled deep inside him; a need to protect her.

That was impossible, of course. When did Seb get involved with a woman who needed anything but sex from him? He *never* promised more and steered clear of any woman whom he thought might have longer-term expectations.

Still, last night had turned out a thousand times better than he'd imagined. He was still musing on that when his phone rang. Seb's brow creased when he saw the caller.

'Sofia?'

'Sebastien, thank God. Please tell me you're still in Vienna. I'm in a scrape and I need your help.'

What was he now, Chief Rescuer of Damsels?

'I've been seeing someone, and I don't know how it happened, but he's started talking love and marriage and—' her voice dropped to a horrified whisper '—*babies*.'

Seb almost laughed. A woman less inclined to settle down than Sofia d'Onzain was hard to imagine. A darker thought occurred. She was the same as he was. Just as determined to stay single and childless.

'He's got in touch to say he's coming over. With something important to say. I think he's going to propose. He's awfully sweet and I don't want to hurt him, but he's not getting the message. Could you come down to my room? Be here when he arrives. And answer the door to him, half-naked or something. Surely, then he'd realise I'm not right for him.'

'You're a grown woman. Just tell him marriage isn't what you want.'

'Don't you think I've tried that? He's determined he can change my mind. *Please*, Sebastien.' He could practically hear her eyelashes batting.

'Okay, if only to save some poor devil from losing his head over the least marriage-minded woman on the continent.'

There were squeals of delight and a babble of effusive thanks, so he raised his voice to make sure she heard his one condition.

'But my shirt stays on, Sofia.'

Agnesse was due to leave the hotel at ten. But by eight she was already showered, dressed, and seated at the desk in her suite, giving her two precious hours to catch up on the work she'd failed to do last night. Her late-evening plans had been thoroughly derailed. A panic attack followed by a night of mind-blowing passion with her former arch-enemy had not been on her agenda.

She'd apologised to Dorel and Christina for kicking them out. She told them she'd been feeling overwhelmed by the events at the gala and needed some time to herself. Neither woman made mention of the guest who *was* allowed into the suite and who'd remained there until 5 a.m.

A tray with a full cafetière and a pretty china cup and saucer sat on her desk. Agnesse rarely ate breakfast. She preferred starting her day with coffee. And the aroma wafting towards her was especially inviting this morning. She took a sip and sighed in contentment.

'Dorel, can we find out which coffee this is, please?'

Her maid, busy with preparations for their departure, paused.

'It's the one we always request,' she said, looking puzzled. 'I checked with the butler.'

Agnesse sipped again, savouring the deep, dark flavours that rolled across her tongue. 'Perhaps it's something about the roast they've used.' It really was superb. 'Will you ask them for a bag or two to take with us?'

Dorel raised a brow but picked up the house phone to relay the queen's request.

In the middle of Agnesse's desk sat her laptop. A manila folder containing the report she failed to read last night was by her left elbow. And to the right, her pen and notebook. Her brow creased. Its elastic closure was twisted. She quickly set it to rights.

There, perfect. Now she could start work.

Yet still, that manila folder lay untouched.

Out on the roof terrace the trees swayed and their leaves rustled faintly in the breeze. Agnesse listened to the pleasant sound as her fingers dawdled across the smooth, polished marquetry of the desk and recalled, with a shivering delight, the astonishing feel of silken skin over rock-hard muscle. With a dreamy sigh, she propped her chin on her hand and studied the floral display on a nearby side table. A bowl of roses in such gorgeous shades of blush and dusky pinks that she couldn't help but smile at them. She'd stayed here on several occasions, but the hotel really had pulled out all the stops for this visit. It had never been quite so enticing before. She was genuinely sorry she was having to leave soon.

'Are we working this morning or daydreaming?' Dorel said with a wry look. 'It's all the same to me but don't expect my sympathy when you get grumpy later about everything left on your to-do list.'

'I do not get grumpy,' Agnesse said, sitting upright then wincing as she felt the sharp pull on tender flesh. The stash of condoms at her bedside had shrunk by three by the time Seb had left her. The man had some stamina. But then, so did she. She'd matched him, pace for pace.

And how she marvelled at that.

Eerik had said she was frigid. She knew now she wasn't. At least not with Seb. The things he made her feel with his hand and his mouth, and his…

She pushed the manila folder away from her. It was pointless. No stuffy old report was going to hold her attention after last night.

'I'll read the morning papers instead,' she announced.

Agnesse usually read a curated selection of stories online, and her maid looked surprised by this break in routine.

'Don't you know that spontaneity is good for the soul, Dorel?'

'Judging by how gingerly you sat in that chair,' Dorel muttered, 'I don't think it was your soul enjoying spontaneity last night.' She collected the newspapers from the sideboard then abruptly dumped several back down again.

'What's wrong with those?' Agnesse said, alerted by the maid's suspiciously innocent expression.

Dorel waved a hand. 'They're far too trashy. They won't be of any interest.'

But Agnesse knew her maid too well to be mollified by that. She pushed to her feet and crossed to the sideboard, gasping in horror when she saw versions of the same story splashed across every front page of the abandoned papers.

Her dreamy recollections of last night evaporated instantly.

They all bore the same photo, which was almost a mirror image of that infamous one. Only this time it was Agnesse staring, frozen in shock, as Seb walked away.

Her hairdo askew, the back of her hand to her burning cheek, her precise emotions at that moment were writ large across her face. Years of careful image management, her father's patient tutoring, had been blown to pieces by fifteen seconds of that playboy's mouth on hers.

Love Struck, read the headlines. *Smooching with the enemy.*

Agnesse threw the newspapers back in the sideboard. Oh, that man! Why did their every encounter have to end in lurid headlines?

Because he turned her into a crazed version of herself. Her mind rebelled at everything he represented while her body couldn't get enough of him.

Events late last night had rather eclipsed the earlier parts of the evening, but looking at that photo brought Seb's behaviour on the dance floor back into searing relief.

Now I think we are even.

He'd rescued her from her panic attack so she could forgive him that kiss—but not the smug expression as he walked away from her. The look of triumph on his face was galling. In their previous altercation, when she'd been the one walking away, at least she'd had the decency to look filled with righteous anger.

At the time, her mother had been furious, of course. But her father, in his usual calm way, had simply asked why she'd done it. When she'd explained he said he could understand why a protective older sister had behaved the way she had, but perhaps she should reflect on it. He couldn't condone violence and he'd asked her to consider the full story, which he was certain Agnesse probably didn't have. Did she really believe the prince would have ever encouraged Isobel? Was his supposed interest not all in her head? *We know*, he'd said with a rueful glance, *what Isobel can be like*.

And after hearing Seb's version of events, Agnesse knew her papa was right.

But he hadn't known about the other thing, about *the smile*…and those cruel, dismissive things she'd heard the prince say about her afterwards. That, as much as Isobel's tears, had made her act the way she had. That and something about Seb himself. Something about the effect he had on her. As if he reached beneath all her careful composure and found the living, breathing woman, not the painstakingly constructed royal image.

Part of her wanted so badly to be found. It was why she'd seduced him.

She'd seduced *him*. She went hot at the thought.

Last night she'd not been Agnesse, the Ice Queen. She'd been another woman entirely. One able to give and receive pleasure. That it happened in the arms of Sebastien von Frohburg was astonishing but also not. The spark had been there from the first time she'd set eyes on him. A spark she'd never felt for another man.

Of course, there was no future in it. Despite what she'd learned about him last night, he was still the unapologetic ladies' man, and hell-bent on pleasure. He could never be the man she needed as her mate through life. If she chose him, she would be choosing most unwisely for Ellamaa. Better to scotch any rumours now before they took hold. The small pang of regret she could live with. But not the disaster of making someone like him prince consort of her people.

The beguiling room and its pleasures had suddenly palled. Even if it meant sitting in her jet on the tarmac for several hours to await their flight slot, she wanted to leave Vienna now.

Christina counselled against using the hotel's main entrance. 'The press are there in numbers, ma'am.'

But Agnesse wasn't going to hide. So Seb had kissed her. So what? If she pretended it was nothing, the press would get bored and move on. The best way to do that was to front it out. Take the positives—that she wasn't made of ice after all—and get on with her life.

The questions came at her as soon as she exited the hotel.

Were she and the prince an item now?

'No.'

Was he a good dancer? Was that a real kiss?

'Yes and no,' she said with her very best regal smile.

Did she know he'd spent the night with Sofia d'Onzain?

She couldn't help it. The smile slipped and her moment's pause was enough for the journalist to pounce.

'Mademoiselle d'Onzain's boyfriend caught them together in her hotel room early this morning. Sofia was barely dressed, apparently.'

The world dipped and swayed. Seb had gone from her bed straight to that of another woman's? How could he? She thought he'd found pleasure in her arms. Was she so disappointing, then? The tightening of her chest almost took her breath.

But she was a Toivonen. They never retreated, nor did they leave the battlefield before delivering the killer blow.

'Where His Highness chooses to spend his time has nothing to do with me,' she said through the lancing pain.

'So you weren't hoping for a relationship with him, then?'

The words spilled out from a place of deep hurt before she could stop them.

'A relationship with Prince Sebastien?' She conjured a tinkle of incredulous laughter for good measure. 'He makes a great show of kissing one woman then takes another to bed in a matter of hours. I'd be scraping the bottom of the dirtiest kind of barrel to have any kind of involvement with the biggest man-whore in Europe. Don't you think?'

She turned her face from the cameras and the rabid interest of the journalists and climbed into the safety of her waiting car before they could see the truth etched across her features.

That somehow she'd permitted Sebastien von Frohburg to upend her life yet again.

The days and weeks that followed were impossibly busy. No chance at all for Agnesse to meet Seb in person and apologise, because if she knew nothing else, she knew that she had to make a heartfelt apology to him.

Even after she'd been rude to him all night and with little provocation from him, he'd come to her aid. Then *she'd* begged him for sex. Not the other way around.

Oh, the sex. The memories of it consumed her. She knew, with every sensible bone in her body, it could never happen again, but that didn't stop her replaying it over and over in her mind. Mostly when she was alone. So that meant at night. When there was absolutely nothing to distract from her need for him. From the longing for his big, hard body in the bed beside her. Some nights it was so bad she could have wept with frustration.

And with shame.

She'd called him a terrible name. In public. So what if he had gone to another woman's bed after hers? He'd made no promises. He wasn't even acting out of type. And he hadn't said a solitary word to the press in retaliation. In one comment on that fateful morning, he'd told a journalist that she'd been a charming companion all evening. The punch? That was long forgotten. And that kiss? He'd overstepped the mark, but she was a beauty, and who wouldn't want to kiss her?

But then they'd repeated the man-whore remark and that she'd said he was beneath her. After that, his replies had all been *no comment*, until he'd disappeared from the public eye altogether.

Agnesse knew she'd wronged him and that this time she had to make amends by apologising.

She could have phoned him. But the moments when she was free never seemed appropriate. Too early in the day. Too late. Who called to make a grovelling apology in a few minutes shoehorned between meetings or in the car heading towards an evening engagement? Her wrongdoing required more of an occasion than that.

A handwritten letter, even an email, appropriately contrite, may have sufficed, and she'd tried, really she had, but every effort had been abandoned before it was ever sent. Nothing short of seeing him in person would do, so he would see the genuine remorse in her eyes. But she knew she was making excuses and as each day passed, she was only making things worse. Then he'd even disappeared completely from public. Which finally drove her to act.

At last, she summoned her courage and rang… Leo.

'Hello, Agnesse.'

'Hi…um…how's…how's Violetta?'

'Violetta?' She heard the bemusement, like he knew she'd meant to say another name and bottled it. 'She's good,' he said. 'She's pregnant.'

Agnesse sensed the pride, the joy, and the love all bundled up in that simple statement.

'I'm so happy for you both,' she said, and meant it. Anyone seeing those two together could not mistake the love they shared. It shone from them. And at last, they were going to be parents. She couldn't be happier for them and was only a little ashamed of the stab of envy and longing at their news. A man to love her, a family of her own, it was what she dreamed of for herself one day. If being the Ice Queen didn't get in the way of that hope. But that wasn't why she'd phoned. She stiffened her spine.

'Leo, I need to see Sebastien. But he's apparently disappeared from the face of the earth.'

'Can you blame him?' There was censure there now, which Agnesse knew she deserved. 'He didn't take those last remarks of yours well. He's not speaking to anyone much.'

'And I'm genuinely sorry for it, Leo. But I need to see him so I can apologise. Properly.'

There was a pause. A prince considering if this queen deserved his help. A fond cousin deciding if he should reveal the whereabouts of his wronged relative.

Eventually, he said, 'Okay. If you really want to see him, I can tell you he's in London. Hiding out at a friend's house. But I'll warn you he's not good company. Snaps your head off at the slightest thing. He may well just fling your apology back in your face.'

Maybe so, but she'd heard a magic word.

London.

She was in Paris. Only an hour or so away, and with a day free of commitments. She could easily be there and back in a few hours with apology delivered, her conscience salved, and hopefully both of them able to move on.

There might never be a better opportunity. She couldn't put it off any longer. She thanked Leo and hung up the phone, then called for her maid and head of security.

'Dorel, you're getting your dream morning. A chance to shop in Paris to your heart's content. But, Christina, we're going to London for the morning.'

CHAPTER SIX

MAN-WHORE.

He'd been called worse and shrugged it off. But Agnesse had believed the worst of him and that had proved harder to dismiss. Why the hell couldn't he move on? It was a month, a whole month, and still he couldn't shake the feeling of regret, the sense that he'd let something of incalculable value slip through his fingers.

Nor the want. He definitely couldn't get that out of his system, and the most unsettling aspect? It wasn't entirely physical. He'd never wanted a woman before for anything other than the obvious. He didn't *need* a woman in his life. So what the hell was wrong with him?

Agnesse represented everything he was determined to avoid—being trapped within the unforgiving hierarchy of a royal family.

He'd thought to divert the strange energies coursing through him by focusing on work. With a laptop and an internet connection he could do that anywhere. Something he'd started as a way to make him financially independent of his father, and the von Frohburg coffers, had grown into so much more.

He'd begun investing at sixteen: start-ups by young people in Grimentz, coffee houses, jewellery designers, fledgling market gardens. Each offered a few thousand euros at most, saved from his allowance. But mostly they worked out and he'd discovered he had an eye for it. He'd branched out, investing more. Bigger, bolder projects: green energy, waste management, as far removed from the realms of a playboy prince as you could get. All done anonymously, so, except for Leo, no one knew. It suited Seb. Let the world judge as it wanted. Let his pompous, elitist relatives continue to see him as feckless and dissolute, beneath them. Because all the while he was amassing a fortune that surpassed any of theirs, that he could wield as he saw fit.

And he was wielding it for good.

After the debacle with Agnesse, he'd tried to bury himself in his work. But Grimentz was a fishbowl and short of locking himself in his rooms, there was no peace to be had from the press.

He'd stayed with a series of friends around Europe, but each time the paparazzi tracked him down. The media wouldn't leave it alone. They were determined there was something between the former enemies.

Yeah, even more enmity.

But Seb maintained a stubborn silence on the matter. Even to Leo, though he knew his cousin had probably guessed. Maybe he'd been right all along. Seb did *like* Agnesse of Ellamaa and maybe that was why it hurt. Not the man-whore insult. With his reputation he couldn't blame her for that. But after their night together, after what they'd done, how they'd talked, that she should still believe without question that he'd gone to another woman's bed? That she'd automatically thought the worst of him? It was that he couldn't bear.

A friend in London was having his Belgravia town house renovated. A planning issue had called a temporary halt to the work, and the property would be sitting empty for at least a week. It was a measure of his state of mind that Seb considered a bare-bones house to be the ideal bolthole. A bed, a bathroom, a fledgling gym in the basement. An annexe out the back for his security team. None of it in the least bit finished yet, but spartan living would suit him.

So he'd thought.

But he hadn't been able to settle. By day, hood up, head down, he'd run incognito through Hyde Park, or hit the basement gym and worked out until he could hardly stand. But the nights were another matter. He'd prowled about the empty house. Restless, confined. On the third night of that torment, he'd gone out.

The bar he'd chosen was cheap and nasty. Perfect for anonymity. Who'd expect a prince to be slumming it in there? Just the place to get blind drunk where no one would notice or care. Except for his security, who'd tried to dissuade him, and when they couldn't, found a table in the shadows and hunkered down to wait it out.

He ignored them, because he was determined to sit there and order whisky until a blonde angel, with a devil's temper and a vicious line in insults, became nothing but a blurred memory.

So it was pure bad luck that the TV in the corner was on a news channel, airing a report about Ellamaa's glamorous young queen and her visit to Paris, the city of lovers, and the lowlife propped at the end of the bar just had to comment.

'City of lovers? She's alone there, though, isn't she? She's a ball-breaker. No wonder she got dumped.'

Seb, nursing drink number seven—or was it eight?—had thrown it back and ordered a refill.

'Needs bringing down a peg, that one. Thinks she's too good for us. Rejecting every man. Look at that poor devil of an ex-fiancé. He practically spelled it out. She's no good in bed.'

The refill went down in one. The empty glass landed with a clatter on the bar.

But the worthless creature hadn't finished. 'Sleeping with Agnesse Toivonen would be like bedding a hunk of frozen meat.'

At that, Seb had got to his feet. He might have staggered as he stood but nevertheless, he'd remembered he'd moved forward, advancing on the owner of that voice. Every instinct in him rebelling against those…those *lies*.

Agnesse of Ellamaa was warm and responsive

and brave and vulnerable. And that vile piece of humanity had dared to even breathe her name.

He'd told him to shut his worthless mouth. Seb had received a punch for his pains and another stream of insults aimed at both him and Agnesse.

After that, the swirling, savage red mist had come down.

Seb couldn't recall many of the details, but in the altercation that followed he knew his security team had gone above and beyond their duty. While he, in contrast and to his everlasting shame, had scraped the very bottom of the filthy, slimy barrel that Agnesse had accused him of inhabiting.

The four-storey town house was swathed in scaffolding. A rubble-filled skip sat concealed behind a neat box hedge. The windows were bare of curtains and the rooms empty of furniture, though paint-strewn buckets and ladders were piled in the centre of the room, visible from the front steps.

Behind Agnesse a line of parked cars ran the full length of the street but otherwise, it was deserted. No one around at all, except for Christina and her team, occupying two vehicles at a discreet distance and ordered by their queen to keep a low profile.

Taking a deep breath, Agnesse rang the doorbell.

She wore skinny jeans and a baseball cap, tugged down to hide her face. She carried a big, flat pizza box emblazoned with the logo of the chain it came from. The same logo was splashed across the back of her hoodie. For all anyone knew, workmen in the house had ordered takeaway.

It may be a fancy part of London, but the house was still essentially a family home and small enough that Sebastien might answer the door himself. But despite ringing twice, no angry sex god appeared. Maybe he was somewhere in the bowels of the house and couldn't hear the door. But Leo had said he was definitely here and she'd come here especially, taking the risk of being spotted. She was prising him out of his hidey-hole whatever.

Agnesse jammed her finger against the bell and kept it there. But when almost a minute later there was still no answer, she admitted defeat and swung away. She'd taken three steps down, when the door flew open.

She opened her mouth to speak but the words died in her throat. This house did have a sex god within and it looked like she'd just got him out of bed.

Sleep-mussed hair. Acres of bare chest. Dressed in nothing but button-up jeans with the top one still undone as if he'd just tugged them on. On this lower step she was at eye level with his hips. A narrow line of chest hairs trailed downward to disappear beneath the waistband into the pieces of his anatomy causing the impressive bulge beneath the button fly. Inconveniently, her own nether regions spasmed in recognition.

'You know it's polite to say hello before you start ogling a man.'

Her gaze swept upward to encounter an expression, chilly as a winter's morning. Then she noticed his jaw sported a bruise. The knuckles wrapped round the door were grazed. There were even angry marks on his arms and torso.

Instinctively, she took a step back up towards him. 'You're hurt.'

He shrugged. 'You should see the other guys.'

Guys? There was more than one. He could have been badly injured; he could have ended up in hospital. Her heart twisted; she could have lost him.

Stupid. He wasn't hers to lose, and judging by his expression he'd prefer her to get lost herself right now.

But then—the relief—he stood aside for her to enter the house. He closed the door behind her and led the way down a long passageway. Past walls of bare plaster and wires, poking out where lamps would be fitted. Into the kitchen space at the back of the house. At its centre was a vast marble-topped island unit. The rest of the space was littered with cupboards and appliances awaiting installation, all still wrapped in their protective coverings.

Here, Agnesse discovered she hadn't got Seb out of bed at all. She'd interrupted his breakfast. On the marble counter was a plate of half-eaten toast, a cafetière of coffee, and a pink mug with its handle missing and bearing the logo Gin o'clock. Where had he found that? Dug it from that skip out front? Such a frivolous thing in his big hand was so incongruous she almost laughed, but she knew if she started she wouldn't be able to stop, and nervous, hysterical giggling would not impress this man.

As she set the pizza box on the counter, he took a swig from the mug. 'What do you want?'

You, she nearly said—battered and bruised, unwelcoming as he was, and now drinking out of that crazy mug. Had she ever seen anything more adorably sexy? How inconvenient that the only man to ever make her heart beat faster could not have been less suitable as husband material, and clearly was not happy to see her.

The knuckles wrapped around the mug looked painful.

'What happened to your hand?' she said, fighting the mad desire to press her lips to them and soothe the hurt.

'A small disagreement,' he said.

'A disagreement that got you hurt? What was it about?'

His gaze clashed briefly with hers. 'It doesn't matter.'

'But you were in a fight?'

A curt nod.

'Where on earth was your security team?'

He sent her a long, level look and remained silent.

He couldn't possibly mean… Her jaw fell open.

'It *was* your security team. I hope they've been fired.'

'Certainly not. They received a substantial bonus and an abject apology from me. I picked a fight with a…' He bared his teeth in a grimace. 'With a worthless lowlife. The team had to step in. Apparently, I took violent exception at their attempts to restrain me.'

'Apparently? You don't remember.' Her eyes narrowed on him. 'You were drunk.'

He stared over her head at the shell of a kitchen with all its swanky appliances still concealed in their packaging. 'I was in need of a crutch. Alcohol fit the bill last night.'

Why did he need that last night? Why did he need a crutch at all? A horrible notion nagged at her. 'Was the fight because of me?' she asked.

His gaze locked on hers and held but he didn't say anything.

And that was answer enough because then she knew. He'd been defending her reputation. Not his. The sting of shame burned like acid in her stomach.

It was well past time for that apology but faced with his hostility and this new, humiliating revelation, her courage failed her. She twisted her hands in the hoodie front. It smelled of the previous owner's perfume, sickly and too sweet. Agnesse's stomach gave a heave.

He watched the movement then tipped his chin at her. 'Where did you get that?'

'From the same place I got the pizza.' She smoothed the front out again. The nausea had passed.

His brow knotted. 'You bought it?'

She chewed on her lip. 'I actually got one of the team to buy it.'

His mug landed back on the counter with such a clatter she marvelled that it remained in one piece. 'How, *buy*?' he said.

'We ordered pizza and when it arrived Christina offered the delivery driver a fifty pound tip for the pizza and the uniform.'

When he stared at her open-mouthed, she added, 'I thought she'd be less intimidating to the girl who delivered it than one of the men on my team. To be fair, Christina was quite reluctant to do it at all.'

'I bet she was. She's one of *the* most recognisable close-protection operatives on the planet, who everyone knows works for you. Whatever you paid that delivery driver it won't be enough. She'll have gone straight to the press. The story will be everywhere by lunchtime. They've probably already got pictures of you dressed like that standing on the doorstep.'

'How could they? I looked like someone delivering pizza. That was the point and no one even knows I'm in London.'

'You can't be that naive. They'll know. They always know where we are.'

'They didn't know *you* were here.'

'They will now,' he said with a glower.

Her chin went up. 'Look, I came all this way and went to all this trouble to apologise for what I said about you to the press.'

'You could have phoned to do that.'

'And would you have taken my call?'

His mouth tightened. Well, that was a no. But she *had* come to apologise and even if he wasn't in a receptive mood, she might as well get on with it.

'I'm sorry. I was in the wrong, but you could be a bit more gracious about it. And you did go straight to the bed of another woman after mine. I wouldn't have minded but you made up some story about not wanting to be seen leaving. That was a lie. You had another date that night.'

'Not true, but you believed it without question.'

'You were *seen*,' she accused him. It had hurt then, and damn but this was hurting her all over again.

'Said who?'

'The press.' She wanted to punch him again. So smug. So calmly standing there when he'd had a second assignation that night. How had she believed that being with her would be somehow different? Once a playboy, always a playboy.

'And they always tell the truth, do they?'

'You were seen in the rooms of Sofia d'Onzain and she was wearing little more than a satisfied-by-Sebastien smile. Isn't that a signature look for your conquests?' she said, nastily, trying to contain all the hurt that was threatening to overwhelm her. Why was she allowing this man to have such power over her?

Emerald splinters flashed in his eyes. 'How is it you claim you're here to apologise and yet once again you're throwing insults at me?'

'You're right. I should never have come. Who you sleep with is none of my business.'

'Then why does it bother you so much?'

'It doesn't.' Though a silly knot of tears was forming in her throat.

He took a step closer. 'And yet, I think if I say one more hurtful thing you'll cry.'

'Nonsense.' She dipped her head, hiding her face beneath the brim of her cap.

He was right in front of her now. 'I did not sleep with Sofia,' he said, lifting her chin with a forefinger so she had to meet his gaze and see the truth there. 'She asked me to make it look as if I had to deter an overeager suitor of hers.'

'Is that supposed to make you sound good? Hurting someone else doesn't exonerate you.'

He was carefully disentangling her ponytail from her cap. The brush of his fingers sent shivers down her spine.

'Trust me. I thought I was doing the man a kindness.' Seb placed the cap on the counter beside her. 'He was the sort Sofia would normally make mincemeat of. The irony is she's the one besotted now.'

He shook his head in disbelief. 'They've even got engaged.'

'Not everyone is as commitment averse as you.'

'I'm not averse to others getting hitched,' he said. 'It's just not for me. I thought it wasn't for Sofia, either. Let's just say the examples we've both witnessed haven't given either of us much confidence in the institution of marriage.'

He sounded oddly wistful, regretful even, and a new and surprisingly painful thought occurred to her.

'Do you love her?'

'Sofia?' He barked in laughter. *'Mon dieu, non.'*

Agnesse nearly slumped in relief. And finally understood then that she'd been fooling herself. The need to apologise in person, while real, had also been a convenient excuse.

She'd been desperate to see him again.

That was what all those sleepless nights had been about. Seb had got under her skin.

'I like Sofia. I sincerely wish her every happiness with her fiancé, and I've no regrets about our times together.'

Agnesse couldn't help it. The words were out before she could question the wisdom of them.

'Do you regret our night together?'

The corner of his mouth titled. 'After all those terrible things you said about me, you mean?' He grazed the back of a knuckle along her cheek. 'No,' he said. 'Not even for a moment.'

He'd meant that gesture as something gentle and soothing, she was sure, but it didn't soothe. It ignited the torch she held for him and sent it roaring into a full-on furnace. The flame he'd first set burning that night in Vienna. No, it went further back than that. He'd set something alight in her all those years ago with that smile of his. As no one else ever had.

Or perhaps ever *could*? And this might be her last time with him. Her last chance to feel again what he made her feel that night.

There was no other way to describe what she did next; she *launched* herself at him. Her mouth, her hands, her ice-maiden's *heart*; she plastered everything she had to him. He staggered a little, caught off balance, until his backside hit the marble counter and he braced against it, using it to keep them both upright.

She didn't notice. She just kissed him, openmouthed and ravenous. Until he hissed in pain.

She pulled back, 'I'm so sorry.'

'No, it's okay, it's just…' He gestured to the bruise. Gentle hands cupped her face, pulling her back towards him. 'Kiss me again.'

She pressed her lips tenderly to the bruise at the corner of his mouth. 'There, is that better?' She took his hands from her face and pressed soft kisses to his grazed knuckles.

She held his gaze and watched it darken. Felt the

sudden shift in his body, the surge of energy, of a new and thrilling tension.

He untangled their fingers so he could snake a hand to her waist, then lower to her behind, so he could press their bodies closer. She heeled off her shoes and they flew to land with a bang against one of the boxes.

Breaking the contact to strip off their clothes was a torment in itself. Who knew where her jeans and panties ended up. They were gone from her and that was all that mattered.

He stripped off the jeans, kicking them away. He lifted her easily onto the counter. The marble was shockingly cold against her naked skin, but then he was there, hot and hard and right where the persistent ache had been since that night in Vienna. She groaned as her head fell back. How much she'd yearned to feel this again.

But…

'Wait,' he said, dragging his mouth from hers. She didn't want to. She spread her legs wider, crushed herself even more intimately into him. But his hands on her hips held her back. *'Wait,'* he repeated.

She was panting and naked in a stranger's kitchen and she didn't care. She wanted him.

'Chérie, we need protection.'

Of course. She hadn't even thought about it.

'I'll be right back.'

She heard him pounding up the stairs and into

a room overhead. It was dispiriting to discover he was prepared, even here, in case a willing female happened along. Did it matter to him that it was her? Could it just have easily been another woman as far as he was concerned? With his history would he really have been celibate this last month?

Then he was back and sheathed and ready, just for her, and she no longer cared about his other women because at that moment he was hers alone.

She was as shameless as the Comtesse d'Onzain and yes, both her daughters. She crooked a finger at him and spread her thighs wider in invitation. Because the comtesse was right; standing there in his naked perfection and fully aroused, Sebastien von Frohburg really was a magnificent beast.

With a growl he strode over to her, possessing her mouth, grasping her hips, and sinking to the hilt in one sublime move. Agnesse moaned in relief. This was what she'd dreamed of every night since Vienna. The hot, hard, remorseless power of him surging into her, her legs clamped about his waist, his hands fisted in her hair. Nothing but his body and hers locked together.

It was fast and furious. Neither of them in control. Just a frenzied coupling in an empty building site of a house. It could have been sordid. But it wasn't. It was exactly what she'd craved. Seb moved her, made her feel things she never had before. But then the doubts crept in. Did he feel the same?

He rested his forehead against hers, chest heaving, catching his breath.

'That was—'

'Good,' she interjected. Fearful she was about to hear 'amateurish' or 'regrettable.' Any of the epithets she was imagining for herself now the glow of release was waning. She'd thrown herself at him twice now. Had any of his other lovers ever been so gauche?

'I was going to say *surprising* but it was good, better than good.'

Surprising how? That he wanted her at all?

He lifted her down and once she moved away to gather her clothes, he retrieved his jeans from where they'd landed, currently adorning a shiny steel fridge. Her own jeans were in a heap on the floor. Her panties two feet away. She grabbed them and tugged them on.

He was dressed before her. Well, back in those jeans at least. The midday sun bounced through the window and glinted in his hair, off his golden skin. Her breath caught.

'We may as well have some of this,' he said, lifting the lid of the pizza box and retrieving a slice. The smell wafted towards her and that nausea came back with such a vengeance she had to fling a hand to her mouth.

They'd passed a cloakroom on the way to the kitchen and she fled there now. Only just reaching it in time. This was the third or fourth time this week.

She'd eaten seafood in a restaurant a few evenings ago. Maybe something had been off.

When she returned to the kitchen Seb's slice of pizza was lying on the counter untouched. 'Are you okay?' He sounded rather more concerned than a bit of mild nausea warranted.

'It's happened a few times over the last week. I think I ate something I shouldn't have.'

'A few times. Could you have picked up a bug?'

'I'm not sure. I've felt a bit off for...' She thought about it. 'Actually about a week. At least.'

'More than a week, then?'

'Yes, now you mention it. Hmm?' She mused aloud. 'So that would have been before the restaurant.'

Seb had gone deathly pale. She frowned at him. 'What?'

'Agnesse,' he said, 'could you be pregnant?'

'Of course not. We used protection. You were most careful.'

'Then when was your last period?'

'Two weeks ago.' Though it had been much lighter than usual, and she'd stopped wearing her favourite perfume because suddenly the smell had become so cloying and then her breasts were rather tender and...and...

The room spun; she felt the blackness coming on. Then nothing but a stream of curses in French and a pair of strong arms grabbing her, lowering her down onto the only chair and pushing her head between her knees.

She couldn't be pregnant. She had things to do. Things to prove. Ellamaa's first ever queen regnant was going to show those doubters how wrong they were.

Was she going to fall at the first hurdle? Who ever heard of a single-parent queen? Oh, God. The wave of nausea and faintness came again.

Seb was by her side again, pushing a glass of water into her hands. She took it and gulped some down.

He'd recovered quicker than she had. He was on the phone, rattling off instructions in French. She heard *pharmacist* and *pregnancy test*.

She focused on getting the room to stop spinning and the basics of staying upright and conscious. One hand clutched the counter; the other was wrapped around her seat.

This couldn't be happening. They'd been careful. But even as she thought that, she knew…she just *knew*.

Since that night something had been slightly off. She couldn't have described exactly how but she'd felt different. She thought it was unrequited lust. Because she'd craved some little piece of Seb that no one else could claim, that she could tuck away in her heart.

He'd left a piece of him lodged inside her all right. Just not in her heart.

The room spun again.

Seb was by her side, placing a damp towel to her forehead, talking to her, telling her it would be all right. How was this going to be all right?

Five minutes later there was a knock on the rear door, and when Seb came back from answering it, he clutched a white paper bag. He pushed his plate and mug aside and unpacked its contents onto the countertop. No less than three identical small boxes. He opened one, scanning the instructions.

'Take this. You'll need to… Well, I guess you might already know what to do.'

'I've not used one before if that's what you mean. But I'll work it out.'

'Do you need help to the bathroom?'

She sent him a glare. She wasn't an invalid. She was a queen and she needed to start behaving like one. Shoulders back, straight spine and if her steps wove in a less than straight line, well, at least she was walking unaided.

The news was the worst.

Agnesse sat on the closed toilet seat in that gloomy room, amidst the part-tiled walls, the window grimy with masonry dust, and wondered if a future monarch had ever announced their presence to the world in such an inauspicious space.

She splashed cold water on her face, tidied her hair then returned to the kitchen, clutching the little white stick with its tiny pink line.

Pregnant.

But behind it all was the thrill. They'd started their own little blip of life. A tiny thing, but hers to love. She was going to be a mother and even the ruinous circumstances couldn't fully extinguish a glimmer of happiness.

The father, in contrast, was grim faced. Not a speck of joy there. Quite the opposite. His look was one of cold resignation overlain with a helping of sheer terror.

'What do we do now?' she asked.

'Considering who we are and who the child will be, I'd thought that was blindingly obvious.' He straightened then gave a small bow. 'Your Majesty, consider this an official proposal. We are getting married.'

CHAPTER SEVEN

HIS PROPOSAL SENT Agnesse staggering towards a seat again. This time she stuck her head between her knees herself. It wasn't the most flattering re-action to the offer of his hand, but Seb supposed he couldn't blame her. He wasn't overjoyed at the prospect himself.

From beneath the tumble of her hair came a plea. 'Can you give me a moment?'

Perhaps he could use one himself. She was okay on that seat. There was really nowhere to fall if she did pass out. Seb quit the room and in the hallway turned to the stairs, taking them three at a time on a burst of restless energy.

Marriage? He nearly stumbled on the last step. But there was no use in regretting his decisions. There was no alternative. He would get on with it and do whatever was required. He pulled out his phone as he strode into the salon at the front of the house.

On the other side of the street was a park. Be-yond the bars of scaffolding caging the front of the house, Seb could see birds flitting busily from tree to tree. Overhead, cotton-soft clouds floated across a sky of clear blue.

He waited for his call to be picked up.

'I'm getting married,' he said as soon as Leo

answered. No point in any preamble. Action was needed now. It might help tamp down the terror he was feeling.

'The Ellamaa Queen, I presume? Congratulations.'

Why did Leo not sound surprised?

'She's pregnant.'

'Ah, I see. Well, a family of your own could be the making of you,' Leo said with absolutely no censure. Actually, he sounded annoyingly upbeat.

'I didn't call for a heart to heart. I called to inform my monarch of my intentions and ask him to be best man.'

'Of course. I'd be honoured. I assume my services will be required sooner rather than later.'

'In the next few days…' Seb inhaled sharply. He'd always told himself he'd never marry. Never risk an emotional commitment to a woman. He'd never wanted to live with the endless fear of things going wrong… How quickly a life could change irrevocably. Well, far better to be in the driving seat when it did. 'As soon as I can arrange everything. Although we won't be announcing the pregnancy yet.'

'Very wise. Make it sound like a love match and not a marriage of necessity.' There was a short silence from the other man, then, 'I hate to ask but it probably needs to be said. You're sure it's yours?'

Seb's quiet 'yes' concealed the blazing need to hit something in lieu of his cousin for suggesting otherwise. Of course the child was his. It never crossed his mind that it wouldn't be. Agnesse was practically a virgin that night. That pitiful excuse of a man who'd called himself her fiancé didn't count, and there had been no other lover since their night together. He'd bet his life on it. He also didn't like the snarling, jealous beast that reared his head at the thought of another man with his hands on her.

'Those photos will be back, of course.' Hell, would they ever. The punch, that kiss in Vienna… Seb could see the prurient headlines now. 'But we'll spin it to our advantage. A classic enemies-to-lovers story.'

'I never knew you could be so romantic.'

'I'm not.' That misapprehension was definitely getting corrected. 'I'm being pragmatic.'

'How's Agnesse with all this?' Leo asked.

Seb thought of her gripping that chair as if her survival depended on it, while her future coalesced around her without input from her.

'She's nearly fainted twice in the last ten minutes, if that's any indication.'

'It's a lot to take in. Marrying the man you're supposed to despise. And dare I ask… How are you?'

There was a squeal from somewhere near Leo and Violetta's excited voice called out, 'He's getting married? Give me that phone.'

'I apologise but apparently my wife would like to speak to you.'

'No, don't, I—'

'Seb? Is it Agnesse Toivonen? *Please* tell me it's her. You two would be perfect together.' She knew that based on what? A punch and a few insults? 'We all saw that kiss. It was hot. You've won her over at last. I knew she'd eventually see what a catch you are.'

'Something like that. Hello, Violetta.' Her boundless optimism usually made him smile. Today, not so much.

'Oops. Judging by my darling husband's face I've just interrupted some serious manly stuff. Bye, Seb. Please bring Agnesse to meet us all soon.'

Leo retrieved his phone again. 'As I was saying… How are you?'

Seb considered that question. Not running for the hills as he might have thought. Amongst the ever-present fear was a sliver of excitement. A father. Him?

He'd not learned much from his own that he could use, except how *not* to parent a child. The man had barely figured in his life at all. When he deigned to grace Seb with his presence, it was only to remind his son of his lowly place in the von Frohburg family hierarchy, and what a curse his arriving at all had been. From his example Seb also knew that giving your heart bore a terrible risk. Leo had been lucky, but Seb was never going there. Yet, neither would he shirk his duty. He'd never condemn another child to the curse of an indifferent father. For better or worse he'd be there for it. For Agnesse, too.

If mother and child even survived...

His gut roiled. What if by getting her pregnant he'd already condemned Agnesse to the same fate as his mother? He crushed that thought before it could take hold.

'Dealing with it,' he said at last.

'Good man. What else do you need?' Leo asked.

'The use of the Mayfair house tonight?'

'It's yours. I'll make the arrangements at this end.' Leo chuckled. 'So Prince Consort of Ella-maa, eh?'

'No. I won't be taking any new titles.' Husband to Agnesse. Father to her child. That would be the extent of it.

'You might like it.'

'No.' He already didn't like the lurking fear of how this might end for Agnesse. He wasn't about to risk any further emotional damage by taking on a royal role that no one wanted him in. Seb the play-boy had been a deliberate choice designed to deflect the offers of any unwanted promotions.

'You'd be *good* at it.' Leo wasn't leaving this alone. He'd make him.

'My father crushed any faith in a royal life out of me. And forgive me, but so did your family.'

'Whether you like it or not, they're your family, too.'

'Don't let them hear you say that. They've spent a lifetime doing their best to pretend I'm not.'

'They may change their minds now you're about to marry into the Toivonens, and the queen, no less.'

'They can all go to hell,' Seb snarled and cut the connection.

At last, the room stopped spinning. Agnesse cautiously lifted her head, but maintained her grip on the chair just in case. She opened her eyes to find she was alone. Seb had given her the space she'd requested. Just as well. It was hard to have any sensible thoughts with his naked torso to stare at. How was it, in the midst of this crisis, her body still craved his? Perhaps it was pregnancy hormones.

Pregnant.

That simple fact had changed everything. The cold, stark reality sank in. Seb was right. There was just one solution for someone like her. Remaining unmarried was unthinkable. Her only option was to marry the father of her baby.

Gone was the chance at love like her parents had shared. That had always been a distant hope. Her duty had to come first, but still there had been a possibility. Not anymore. Seb did not love her, nor was he the kind of man to develop those feelings in time. He'd been pretty clear about that. She supposed she should be grateful he believed in duty, at least.

Time to find him and accept his proposal.

His voice came from the floor above. She followed the sound and found him at the front of the house. In a room that would one day be a glamorous lounge with a pretty view of the park on the other side of the street.

Now the only thing lending the bare room any glamour was the stunning, shirtless man standing at the window. His back to hers, arms folded across his chest, legs planted wide, he looked like a warrior ready to take on the world.

He'll keep us both safe, she thought. *Me, and this little one.* Her hand went to her belly.

Seb's head swung towards her, his gaze dropping swiftly to where her hand rested.

'Are you all right? I wasn't too rough before?'

Oh, all that concern in his stormy green eyes. It warmed her to her very soul. She nodded. 'Who were you speaking to?'

'Leo. I was asking if he'd be my best man.' Uncertainty clouded his expression. 'If I require one?'

Agnesse swallowed hard. What other choice did she have? 'Yes, I'll do it.'

His look of relief was so profoundly different to the tension of moments before. When he stretched out his hand to her, she went to him at once, her feet carrying her towards him of their own accord. Her body simply couldn't resist him. And the warmth of his hand as it engulfed hers was so comforting that she didn't hesitate when he drew her closer into his embrace and kissed her. A slow, sweet, drugging kiss that mightn't be about love but still had a tantalising air of romance about it.

When he lifted his head at last, she opened her eyes to gaze up at him. But he was looking elsewhere, to the street below and with a determined and decidedly unromantic expression on his handsome face. She glanced in the same direction and saw movement. There was a lone figure on the far side of the street. With his camera lens pointed directly at them, a photographer stood snapping shot after shot.

Seb tightened his grip on her, took her jaw firmly in hand so she couldn't move as he looked down on her.

'So our story begins. We fell in love. We tried to fight it but it's too strong for either of us. We met in secret but alas, we've finally been discovered.'

Love? Wrapped in his arms like this, the absolute focus of those burning green eyes, she feared that it would be all too easy to fall deeply for him. But would those feelings ever be reciprocated? She freed her chin and turned her cheek to his chest, feeling shaky again. This would be a marriage of convenience only. Of lust, yes, but not love, and she would do well to remember it.

'How will anyone believe that?' she said.

'Easily, if we feed them the right images. And when the baby comes and they realise you were already pregnant when we married, it will still be seen as a love match and that the child is…' His voice caught. 'That this child is wanted and loved.'

Beneath her cheek his heart beat a furious tattoo and she knew in that, at least, he meant every word. Then he slid a hand into her hair and tilted her head back, angling her face up towards him.

'Now, kiss me again and look like you mean it.'

His mouth came down on hers in an all-consuming kiss so profound that Agnesse didn't have to pretend. She couldn't help it. She was lost in him.

Thirty minutes later they were gathered in the hallway. One of Seb's team, with a bruised jaw to match his employer's, stood poised to open the front door. Behind them were the remainder of the team, carrying various pieces of luggage, and between them sporting a selection of split lips and black eyes. They'd clearly shown commendable restraint in saving their royal charge from himself last night.

Outside, Christina waited with Agnesse's protection detail, keeping the press back from the front steps. That single photographer had been joined by two dozen more journalists.

Agnesse had replaced the pizza uniform with the navy blazer she'd been wearing that morning when she'd left Paris. But she almost wished she were wearing one of Seb's sweats. It would have swamped her, but she wouldn't have cared. She'd have happily hidden away inside it completely and never come out again.

Seb was devastatingly handsome in a sharp charcoal suit and white shirt, open at the neck. She could barely drag her eyes from him.

'Ready?' he asked her.

For what awaited them on the other side of that door? The scandal, the scrutiny, the disapproval of her prime minister. Her sister's surprise. Her mother's disappointment. And marriage to this man?

Hardly.

But his arm was a protective shield about her; his body her safe haven as he tucked her in under his shoulder and their joint teams cleared a path through the jostling cameras and baying journalists.

'You're loved up now but what about that punch?' one of them shouted.

'All forgotten,' Seb answered, flashing a brilliant smile for the cameras.

'By the look of that bruise she's been at it again.' A ripple of humiliating laughter ran through the pack around them.

Agnesse turned her face into the wall of his chest, grateful for her big paparazzi-proof sunglasses. She knew her eyes would have instantly given her away. Unlike him, she could not have put on a show. Everyone would have seen the bald shock and they'd have surely guessed the calamitous truth.

Pregnant.

By this man. Who was insisting they marry.

Would her people believe she'd fallen at the first hurdle? Thinking she was imposing the most unsuitable of prince consorts on her country, a man whose only real achievement, they'd think, was seducing half the women of Europe.

'It's an odd location for a romantic tryst. Why were you here?'

'Privacy,' Seb told them over her head. 'We thought we'd escaped notice, but you found us anyway.'

'That pizza stunt was a dead giveaway. Were you hoping to be discovered so you could force him, Agnesse? You want the man-whore after all?'

She missed her footing on the kerb, but Seb was there, supporting her, helping her into the backseat of the car, then following her in. The door slammed shut against that mob outside. She sat there, numb, unable to move, and he leant over to fasten her seat belt. Now they'd left the sanctuary of the house, this had all become so real.

'Agnesse,' he said, gently taking her chin in his hand. 'Breathe.'

For all its softness, that command could not be disobeyed. Her body responded. Air whooshed through her teeth; her lungs expanded.

He was the captain of her stricken life and he'd just saved her from foundering on the rocks. But how, *how* could she go through with this?

'I don't think I can marry you, after all,' she said, weakly.

'It makes no difference. I'm the father of your baby and I'm staying at both your sides.'

Her body thrilled to that even though her mind and heart rebelled.

He doesn't love you. He'll never love you.

'What if it's not yours?' she said, breathless and panicky, and suddenly desperate to find a way out.

He turned angry green eyes on her. 'Are you telling me you've been with someone else in the last month? You'd play that old trick, would you? Foisting another man's child on the poor sap who'd marry you because he believes in duty?'

'No, of course not.' She sank down in her seat. Ashamed of herself. He hadn't questioned that the child was his. Believing in her straightaway. Which was more than she'd done for him in Vienna. Was Sebastien von Frohburg, the louche playboy, actually an altogether different kind of beast? An honourable man?

It was a short drive to the von Frohburgs' London residence. Agnesse's base was in Paris and she had no home here. Otherwise, she would have insisted that was where they went. Though it might have fallen on deaf ears.

'You should rest when we get to the house. Give me a few hours to arrange everything.'

'Everything?'

'The wedding.'

'Wedding?' This was moving too fast. She swayed forward in her seat, but he flung out an arm to stop her toppling.

'The sooner I get you home, the better.'

'Home?' she repeated.

Oh, for Heaven's sake. Had pregnancy turned her into a parrot now?

'Ellamaa. The Summer Palace, to be precise. What could be more appropriate than taking your new fiancé home to meet your family?' His hand hovered just in front of her, a precaution in case she swayed again. 'You said it's the one place you can truly rest. A pregnant woman needs to take care of herself.'

'But I will still have things to do,' she argued. 'I'm the queen.'

Yes, she was. And it was time for her to start behaving as one. She couldn't let him take over this way.

'You're pregnant with my child,' he said. 'That supersedes everything else.'

The hell it did. She stiffened her spine. 'I won't agree to this.' But she was protesting to an empty space. They'd arrived under the portico of Leo and Violetta's London home. Seb was already out of the car and was crossing to her side.

'I can manage,' she said crossly, refusing the hand waiting to help her out.

'I'd be more convinced of that if you didn't look like you were about to faint at every comment I make.' He followed that up by clamping her to his side as they walked into this new address.

If Seb's temporary bolthole had been a luxuri-ous London home in the making, the official London residence of His Serene Highness, the Crown Prince of Grimentz, was a fully-fledged, statement-piece palace, with marble staircases, crystal chandeliers, and priceless artwork everywhere she looked. She spied at least one Tintoretto hanging in a reception room and a pretty little Vermeer landscape peeked out from a corner of the hallway.

This wasn't a family home, at least not the ground floor. It was designed to demonstrate the wealth and status of its owners. Was this what Seb had grown up with? How different would he find the Summer Palace? There were treasures there, and in her family's other homes across Europe, but mostly the emphasis was on luxurious comfort and ease.

The butler and housekeeper greeted them warmly. It was obvious there was genuine affection for Seb. They *liked* him. They fussed over him, anxious about his cuts and bruises. He brushed that off and he greeted them like old friends.

Then at word from Seb, the housekeeper was whisking Agnesse away to a guest suite and he was disappearing into one of the salons, his phone clamped to his ear and barking out commands in French.

The rooms she was shown to were as grand as the rest of the house, though they were divinely comfortable. Agnesse sank down into a silk-upholstered couch. Grateful to sit. Despite what she'd told Seb, she was still feeling wobbly.

But it was time she made a call of her own. Her

mother should be informed, and Agnesse sorely needed to hear her voice right then.

Mathilde Thiset-Toivonen could be tough on her children, but then she wasn't just a mother; she was a queen, too, with all the demands that entailed. Agnesse knew it was her way of helping her children navigate the inescapably public lives they'd been born into. When they erred, they might be subjected to a thorough dressing down but in the end she was always there for them, no matter what they'd done. Just as she'd supported her husband throughout his reign. His 'rock' he'd called her. Agnesse wanted to find a similar partner in life. Would Seb be that for her? She certainly couldn't fault his reaction to her pregnancy so far. Maybe her mother would be impressed with that. She might even like Seb. If she gave him a chance.

The phone was answered on the second ring.

'Agnesse, what's this I hear about you being in London with that dreadful womaniser?'

So much for Mathilde liking her future son-in-law.

'I came here to apologise for the terrible things I'd said about him in Vienna.'

'I'm sure you didn't say anything he hasn't heard before, and whilst you might have been a little uncouth, you essentially spoke the truth.'

But she hadn't. She'd been mistaken, about his night with Sofia and perhaps more than that. Hadn't he proposed to her in a heartbeat? Was that the behaviour you'd expect of an irredeemable playboy?

Agnesse steeled herself for the next part. 'He's asked me to marry him and I've… I've said yes.'

'Marry that man?' her mother stuttered. 'Why on earth—'

'Mama, I'm pregnant.'

The silence was mercifully short, and her mother's observation when it came had no judgement in it.

'In that case, my darling,' she said on a sigh, 'you'd better come home as soon as you can.'

CHAPTER EIGHT

HER FUTURE HUSBAND sat still and silent beside her. His gaze was fixed on the view unfolding beyond the car window; his first glimpse of the grounds of the Summer Palace.

And his new home.

He'd have a harder time taking charge of everything here than he had in London. Whisking her to the von Frohburgs' London residence. Organising her staff, who'd fallen in with his plans far too readily. He'd made sure she ate something, told her to rest, even charming Dorel, whom he'd had flown from Paris, into obeying his commands.

'Traitor,' she'd muttered as her maid had hurried to do his bidding. Dorel had shrugged and done it anyway.

They'd left Mayfair in the early hours. Seb arguing that they should travel through the night to be with her mother by morning, and before the story broke properly in that day's news schedules.

He'd hustled her onto the plane—*her* plane—and ushered her straight to the bedroom, where he'd insisted she got into bed. Then promptly left her. She'd been too wrung out to argue, falling asleep the moment her head hit the pillow.

What Seb had done on the three-hour flight was anyone's guess. When he'd woken her twenty minutes before landing, he'd looked as fresh faced and in control as when she'd closed her eyes.

Agnesse desperately wanted to know what he was thinking now as his new home appeared before them. One not really of his choice. He was only marrying her out of his sense of duty. How different might this homecoming have been for them both had there been any love involved?

The physical attraction was there. She'd happily ravish him on the plump leather seats of this stately limo. Despite the driver and security sitting up ahead. She sighed in frustration and instantly Seb's head swung towards her.

'Is everything all right?' There was an anxious glance, an all too fleeting brush of his hand, but there wasn't a flicker of heat in it. If there was, he'd tamped it down so well it was completely hidden. The ache of lust and longing had become all hers, apparently.

The familiar landscape slipped by. The parkland with its ancient trees, the deer grazing at the edge of the lake. Her home itself was partly obscured by a haze that often rose from the lake in the summer months. It would clear in an hour or two but until then, only the upper stories were visible, floating, as if by magic, above the tendrils of mist. The palace's pale lemon walls and white-tiled sloping roof were dazzling in the early-morning sun.

'Ellamaa,' Seb said, softly. 'The land of fairies.'

Agnesse knew her principal home was nothing

like the one he grew up in—a hulking fortress built primarily to keep its owners safe and intimidate its enemies.

Not this elegant palace. Yes, created to impress visitors but still more, made for the pleasure and comfort of its occupants, with its formal gardens and sprawling parklands, its sumptuous staterooms and forty bedrooms. The von Frohburgs of Grimentz might be fabulously wealthy, but for comfort and sheer beauty the principal residence of the Queen of Ellamaa knocked their forbidding fortress into a cocked hat.

She'd always loved this approach to her family's home. On mornings like this it could take her breath away.

Their car turned into the drive that would take them to the private entrance used by the family. It took them past the east wing, past the grounds remodelled by her father where he'd had the parklands restored to a wildflower meadow. Protected by a deer wall to keep them safe from the grazing livestock, a sea of poppies and daisies ran uninterrupted to the tree line. Her father would have loved it.

They passed the end of the wing where the chapel was situated. Tomorrow, if Seb had his way, the archbishop would conduct their marriage in its hallowed space, with Leo and her mother standing witness.

Leo was arriving tomorrow. Along with Sebastien's hastily packed possessions.

'Wouldn't you have wanted to oversee that yourself?' she'd asked him as they'd climbed onboard the jet in London.

'It's fine,' he'd said with a shrug. 'I don't have much.'

And her heart had squeezed. Who *was* this playboy prince with apparently so little to his name?

Keert was waiting for them at the family entrance. Agnesse made the introductions. Her secretary bowed low then looked startled when one hand landed on his shoulder and another grasped his in a firm shake.

'The secretary famous for seamless organisation. Your reputation precedes you,' Seb said with a broad smile. 'You're the envy of royal households across Europe.'

Completely disarmed, Keert stammered his thanks. The next introduction was more frosty.

The dowager queen awaited them in her private sitting room. Seated on an elegant chaise, she rose in all her state as they entered. There was a warm embrace for her daughter. The interloper received a haughty glare and the barest fingertip stretched out for him to take. 'You must be Sebastien.'

'Your Majesty,' he said, bowing over her hand and adding that heel click that Agnesse found so… so *distracting*.

'Forgive me, ma'am,' he said, slewing a glance to a painting hanging to one side of the fireplace. 'But is that a Raphael?'

Her mother's gaze flickered to the portrait of

a golden-haired Madonna. 'It is. My late husband gave it to me on our last anniversary.'

Seb studied the canvas in open admiration. 'It's a very fine piece. He had excellent taste, ma'am.'

'Yes, he did.' Mathilde's gaze softened as she studied the painting, then she turned away and drew Agnesse down to take a seat on the sofa beside her. She did not invite Seb to sit.

'I've arranged for you to see the family physician. He'll be here later this morning,' her mother said, ignoring Seb still standing politely.

'Can't it wait a day or two?' Agnesse asked, not wanting to be prodded and poked. 'I've taken a pregnancy test. I think it's clear.'

'I know, my darling—' her hand went to her daughter's cheek '—but you're planning such a big step. Let's be absolutely certain about everything.'

'Your mother is right, Agnesse. It's wise to be seen by your own doctors as early as possible. So they can monitor how you and the baby are doing.'

At Seb's words, her mother's lip curled, as if she was fending off an unpleasant smell. 'Quite,' she said.

At last, Mathilde waved a hand, indicating that Seb should sit. Agnesse watched transfixed as he undid the button on his jacket and sank gracefully into the sofa opposite. But she couldn't mistake the expression. Her fiancé was being polite but beneath the elegant manners, she sensed the steel and determination. Her mother might have met her match.

'I've had a request from Grimentz Castle for a visit by the crown prince tomorrow. I have, of course, said yes on your behalf, Agnesse. But really, does the marriage have to be quite so hasty?' She took her daughter's hand and stroked it.

'Ma'am,' Seb cut in. 'There seems to be little point in delaying. A small, quiet wedding would not be inappropriate during the period of official mourning, and the sooner Agnesse and I are married, the better it will appear once the pregnancy is announced.'

'And is that the life you want, young man? Forever standing two paces behind my daughter? Because, make no mistake, that will be the reality of your position. Even if you are the prince consort, there will be no transfer of power to you.' She sounded so angry but what else did her mother think could happen? Was she hoping Seb would change his mind? Because that would be disastrous. Agnesse couldn't raise their child alone. She and Seb were tied together even if protocol demanded he stand a hundred paces behind her.

'I assure you, power is the last thing I want. In fact, I won't even be taking the title.'

Her mother swivelled towards him in surprise. 'But it would be expected of you.'

'I'm sorry, I should have apprised Agnesse of this sooner, but I have no desire for a formal royal life. I will of course support my wife in any way I can, but as husband only, not as consort.'

'In our world there in no difference,' her mother said, angrily. She turned back to Agnesse. 'And if you think there is, you can both explain that to the prime minister. He's requested an audience with you. Keert has made the space in your diary after lunch.'

Seb's declaration was a bombshell. She was already marrying a man with a problematic reputation, and now he'd revealed he had no intention of supporting her by taking a formal role. How was Agnesse expected to explain that to her prime minster? A stuffy traditionalist who already believed she wasn't up to the job of being queen.

'Does he know about the baby?' Agnesse asked. God forbid she'd have to discuss that with him, too. She was already imagining his disapproval and attempts to retain some control over her once he knew she was about to take a husband. How would he react if he knew there was a child conceived out of wedlock, too?

'Of course not. There is no need for anyone to know yet. It's too early. You're barely a month gone. When the time comes you could say it's a honeymoon baby.'

Agnesse dismissed that idea. 'People can do maths, Mama. Besides, I don't have time for a honeymoon.' She ran a mental tally of the work she'd already delayed over the past two days. She couldn't afford to fall any further behind.

Her mother shot a disapproving glance in Seb's

direction, as if she wasn't surprised her daughter didn't want to spend any time with him.

'Until things are settled, for the prince tonight I thought the Rose guest suite.'

Agnesse silently added 'would do' because surely that was what her mother had meant.

'It can be changed of course if it doesn't suit. But it seemed sensible as you may choose not to stay at all.'

Seb stood, fastened the button on his jacket, and advanced towards their sofa. 'You could house me in the stables if you want, ma'am,' he said with a martial gleam in his eyes. 'But I assure you, I'm staying.'

He took Agnesse's hand, lifted it to his lips. The touch sent a shimmer of need over her skin.

'I will leave you to talk with your mother, Agnesse. I'll find a servant to direct me to my rooms. Your Majesties,' he said, and with a formal bow and click of his heels he quit the room.

Her mother's eyes narrowed on the doorway through which Seb had departed.

'I can see how you might have been seduced by him. But if he thinks all will be forgiven with fine manners and a few pretty compliments about your father, he is very much mistaken.'

After lunch, during which she ate almost nothing—and despite Seb's best efforts to pile tempting morsels on her plate—Agnesse settled in the Prince Josef salon to await the arrival of her prime minster.

They met regularly, but today she'd dressed especially carefully. A fitted, knee-length dress in sombre grey, pearl earrings, her father's mourning medal, and grey leather pumps with five-inch heels. Royal power dressing at its best.

She wished Seb could have joined her from the start, but he'd declined.

'You can do this,' he said with a kiss to her cheek. 'And I'll be there as soon as you need me.' And off he went to wait in the adjoining salon.

From the corridor she heard Keert greeting her guest.

Andris Nilsson had served as head of government for the past decade. She'd been fourteen when he'd arrived at the palace for his first audience with the king. Despite all the intervening years, he couldn't see that she was a grown woman. He was frequently patronising, and since her accession had tried to control her, doing what he could to constrain the changes she wanted to make in her role.

The door opened. After making his usual bow, which was never quite as deep as the one he would have made to her father, the prime minister strolled towards her. 'Your Majesty, how lovely you look today. Quite the young lady.'

I'm twenty-five, she wanted to snap, but held her tongue.

'Prime Minister,' she said, rising to shake his hand.

He took hers in both of his and held on. 'Now, what is this I hear about some hastily concocted marriage plans, hmm? I'll convene the cabinet and we'll discuss it next week.'

'By all means, but you were informed as a courtesy only.' She reclaimed her hand and returned to her seat, waving him to a seat facing her own. 'I'm not asking your permission. I don't need it.'

'Ma'am, you're young and, forgive me, rather inexperienced.' He was still standing so she was obliged to look up at him. Giving him an advantage. No doubt as he intended. 'I must advise caution. His Highness, Prince Sebastien, is a foreign national, after all.'

'Yes, from Grimentz. With whom we share a deep and abiding friendship. My father and the crown prince were great friends.'

'With all due respect, you're not marrying the crown prince.'

'I should hope not. His wife would have something to say about it.'

Her country's senior official did not smile at that. In fact, his expression hardened. 'Your father would have counselled you against this union.'

'No, he would not. He would have trusted my judgement. And I'm not ignorant of the protocols. I would only need your permission if I were marrying an individual from a hostile state or whose position may be thought to outrank mine.'

At last, he sat. 'Ma'am, I think you know what I'm really trying to say here.' He sent her an oily smile that set her teeth on edge. 'Prince Sebastien's reputation is a cause for concern. I do wish you'd allow yourself to be advised by those older and wiser.'

'And I wish you would recognise that I'm perfectly capable of making this decision myself. The prince is not the man you think he is. He has qualities and depths beyond those the world chooses to see.'

He snorted. 'Oh, he has hidden depths all right. I had hoped to spare you this, but as you appear determined to run headlong into this mistake, I must tell you some shocking images have recently come to light.'

He drew a series of photographs from a file he carried. Blown-up, grainy images of a grubby back alley, where Seb wrestled with three men, who were restraining him while he bared his teeth at someone out of shot. A second showed her fiancé throwing a drunken punch. Another caught him flailing while he was forcibly bundled into the back of a car.

'These were taken only the other night. Your fiancé was involved in a street fight. A common brawl, ma'am. And one that he started because he was intoxicated, I'm told. I am deeply shocked by these behaviours. How can you possibly believe this man suitable to be prince consort of Ellamaa?'

'I know of this incident, Mr Nilsson. The prince

has explained the circumstances to me. And my intentions have not changed.'

His brows lowered and he leant forward in his seat, like a bull about to charge.

'You would still take him as husband, after learning about this and what else besides? A drunk, a known womaniser to boot? One might, respectfully of course, wonder have you taken leave of your senses, young woman?'

'No, but I think you may have taken leave of your manners, Mister Nilsson,' Agnesse said, never taking her gaze from his. 'May I remind you that I am your queen.'

The prime minister flushed red. 'Forgive me, ma'am.'

Agnesse continued, 'While I do not condone his behaviour, I cannot condemn the intention behind it. The prince had already informed me about this incident. He was defending my reputation and was prepared to suffer harm to do so, even after all he'd received from me was shameful insults. Could you say the same, Prime Minister?'

She was done with diminishing Sebastien von Frohburg.

'So you are determined to marry this…this brawling prince?' The prime minister nodded towards the photographs.

'I have found the man I…love.' She could say that because it was important. 'One I believe will support me in my role. Naturally, I have taken the advice of my mother.' Who probably shared the prime minister's misgivings though Agnesse wasn't going to tell him that, and she knew with a certainty, neither would the dowager queen. 'But in the end, the decision about whom I would marry was only ever going to be mine.'

'You would elevate such a creature to the lofty position of consort?'

A creature? Seb was a *man* of principle and kindness and duty. Agnesse lifted her chin and held her ground. Seb deserved all the protection she could give.

'Actually, my future husband will not be taking the role of consort. He has no interest in the trappings of status and power. Instead, he has stated his desire to continue to live a private life.'

The prime minister's jaw tightened in disbelief. 'Then what, may I ask, is he going to do with his time?' His voice was rising to a disrespectful volume. 'Run around whoring again?'

'I'll be doing whatever Her Majesty asks of me.' Seb's cool voice came from behind her. Even without that, Agnesse would have known he'd just entered the room. The look of astonished fury on the minister's face was priceless.

'I understood our conversations were private, ma'am,' he growled. 'At least they were in the old king's day.'

Seb's hand arrived on her shoulder. Agnesse felt the subtle squeeze of support and allowed her fingers to float up and settle over his, more grateful than she could say for his solid presence.

'Tell me,' Seb said, 'did you attempt to bully and brow beat the old king, too? Because from where I was sitting, I heard little respect for your monarch.'

The man huffed and blustered but didn't answer.

Agnesse rose to her feet, signalling the meeting was at an end.

'By all means, Prime Minister, if you think it will be in Ellamaa's best interest, release those pictures,' she said. 'But you should know that it won't change my decision.'

It couldn't. She carried Seb's baby. But it surprised her to discover that regardless of that, she'd still mean it. Her fiancé was a good man.

He glared at Seb, his mouth twisting when he spotted the bruise to his jaw.

'Very well, ma'am. You have made your intentions clear. I can only hope you won't come to regret it.'

With a fleeting bow for her and nothing at all for Seb, the prime minister spun on his heel and stalked out.

'Perhaps we shouldn't have done that,' Seb said when the door closed and they were alone again.

'Yes, we should. Odious man. Because I'm young and female he thinks he can push me around. That's not how my father raised me. It's time the prime minister got used to that idea.'

She felt good. That was the first time she'd properly stood up to him.

'Thank you for defending me,' he said, 'but I'm sorry about those photographs.'

'I'm not. It's made him show his true colours at last. He doesn't respect me. It's useful that I finally know that for certain. But he won't release them. It would be seen as an attack on the monarchy. He's already losing popularity and that might weaken his position further.'

'It's pretty certain someone else will, though, and it's going to cause a world of trouble for you.'

'I don't care. I know that's not who you are. And you should let others see the real you sometimes.'

He spread his hands wide. 'But I do,' he said with that lazy smile of his.

She narrowed her gaze. She wasn't fooled. She knew he'd just retreated behind the persona of the playboy prince. She could see the difference now.

The family was to gather for dinner. Her mother suggested it was the perfect opportunity for Isobel and Carl to meet their new brother-in-law before the wedding.

'As you both seemed determined you are going through with this,' she said to Agnesse as they waited in her sitting room for her other children and Seb to arrive. 'I heard that the prime minister was practically puce when he left you both this afternoon. I wish I'd been there to see you stand up to him at last. Though Sebastien also played a part, I hear.'

God bless Keert for sharing that. Her mother needed help seeing past Seb's former reputation.

'I was supposed to be dining with friends in the city tonight.' Isobel burst through the door, in skin-tight jeans and a protest T-shirt. 'But after all those photos of you and a naked Sebastien von Frohburg practically broke the internet, I had to stay at home and discover all the juicy details.'

'Naked?' Mathilde said in alarm as Isobel crossed the floor to gather her sister in a hug.

'He was missing his shirt, that's all,' Agnesse quickly reassured her.

'Didn't look like that in the clinches I saw.' Isobel bent to kiss her mother on both cheeks. 'And I thought I was the scandalous one in this family.' She plonked down beside her sister. 'So where is he?'

'On his way. Be nice, Issy, won't you?'

'You know me. I'll be charming,' she said, all innocence.

'Like the last time, you mean? When you convinced me he'd broken your heart?'

She had the grace to look at least a little contrite.

'I'm sorry, Ness. I wasn't being truthful,' she said with a rueful smile. 'He'd actually been sweet to me when, you know, I'd probably been a bratty teenager.'

'But I punched him, Issy.'

'I know. Go you.'

Agnesse threw up her hands. 'No, it's not *go me*. I'm so ashamed. It was a terrible thing to have done.'

'But it's all worked out okay because you're getting married.' Isobel flashed her an angelic smile. 'So tell us. How long have you been secretly seeing him?'

'I haven't. That time in Vienna was our first meeting in years.'

'He got you pregnant after one night?' Isobel whistled. 'He should have *stud* tattooed on his forehead?'

'He should have a health warning tattooed somewhere,' Agnesse muttered. 'But I wasn't thinking of his head.'

Her sister's eye widened in interest.

'Big, is he? Like being impaled on an elephant trunk?'

'Isobel,' their mother scolded. 'A little decorum, please.'

'Come on, Mother. We're all grown women in here. Surely, you know what I'm talking about?'

After a moment a wash of colour stained Mathilde's cheek and a smile played at the corner of her mouth. 'Well, your father was rather…well made.'

Isobel snorted. Agnesse blushed. Then mother and daughters dissolved into laughter. Exactly at the moment Seb walked in.

'Oh, look,' Isobel said with a wicked glance at her sister. 'It's the head of the herd.'

That comment and Seb's adorable, frowning confusion had Agnesse laughing so hard she had to stuff a handkerchief in her mouth. It was nerves or stress or baby hormones. Maybe all three. She wasn't normally so unrestrained. She peeked up at Seb. Or perhaps it was something about her soon-to-be husband. He was dressed in a navy suit and matching shirt and looked good enough to eat. Agnesse's mouth went dry.

Isobel saved her by getting to her feet to greet her future brother-in-law.

'Sorry for being a nightmare and causing all that trouble. No hard feelings, and welcome to the family,' she said, lifting up on on tiptoe to peck Seb's cheek. 'And be good to my sister, or else.'

As apologies went, Seb supposed it covered the essential points, but Isobel Toivonen appeared to be as much a force of nature as ever.

Whilst she didn't have the delicate, arresting beauty of her elder sister, she was a handsome young woman with a vivacity about her that drew the eye. Seb could understand how she could break hearts and cause all the turmoil that dismayed her mother and filled the gossip columns. And he would forgive her much of that when he saw how devoted she appeared to be to her sister. They'd had their heads together, giggling over some joke, as he walked in. He got the impression he was the butt of it; not that he cared if it brought him the sweet pleasure of hearing Agnesse's unrestrained laughter.

But then she stared up at him with hungry eyes and the rest of the room faded away. She'd defended him earlier. Standing up to her country's chief government official. Apart from Leo, who'd ever done anything like that for him? Seb had been moved.

Then she'd urged him—*let others see the real you*.

Not likely. Never had, never would. Except in that moment he'd had the alarming impression that she was beginning to see precisely that. Curiously, he still wasn't quite sure how he felt about it.

The youngest of the siblings stuck his head round the door. Carl, who in most other royal families of Europe would have been king now instead of his elder sister holding the title of queen.

He kissed his mother, hugged both his sisters, but appeared completely star-struck as Seb put out his hand.

His handshake was firm but his greeting was mumbled and after that, he fell silent, leaving the conversation to his older sisters. Which meant mostly Isobel. She peppered Seb with questions about Grimentz. About Leo. About his views on world events.

'Isobel, for Heaven's sake,' Agnesse scolded. 'Let the man draw breath, will you?'

All the while Carl had watched and listened and

used the sudden silence to finally find his voice, asking the one thing that at least sixty percent of those present would have preferred he had not.

'So are the stories about your conquests true?'

Seb wasn't responding to a question like that. Not with his future wife and mother-in-law present. He'd hoped his raised brow might have prompted the young man to change the subject. Unfortunately, Carl took it for affirmation and slapped his thigh in glee.

'I knew it. Oh, you absolute player.'

Mathilde inhaled sharply while Agnesse dropped her head into her hands on a groan.

'Whatever happened in the past,' Seb said, 'a wise man knows when to move on. We learn, we find new loyalties, new alliances. And the past stays firmly where it belongs.'

That right there was a lesson in diplomacy if the impertinent boy was able to see it. The blush and hurried apology suggested that he had. Perhaps the young man had potential, after all.

'Thank you, Sebastien. That was most informative,' Mathilde said, rising abruptly to her feet. 'And on that note, let's go in to dinner, shall we?'

CHAPTER NINE

IF THE DOWAGER QUEEN had meant to insult him with her choice of guest rooms, her intention had missed the mark. Seb found them to be perfectly comfortable and had quickly discovered that the feminine-sounding Rose suite was in fact named for its garden view and not for its decor, which was a restful mix of blue and ivory.

Perhaps the intended insult resided in the distance between his quarters and that of his fiancée's. Any clandestine visit would have required directions from a passing footman, and even then would have taken some time to accomplish. The Rose suite appeared to be as far from the family wing as possible.

Not that he'd had any intention of seeing his bride last night. While she was pregnant he was going to be extremely careful when, or even *if*, he touched her again. Yes, he knew the science; his rational brain knew the risk would be minimal if he made love to her. But knowing and actually *believing* it would be okay were two different things in his world—a world where his mother had lost her life and his father had then lost the ability to care for anything.

Last night's dinner and Seb's introduction to his new family had been surprising. He'd expected strained conversation and inevitable silences. But the family had been relaxed from the start.

He'd made it his particular business to draw the mother out.

She rebuffed most of his attempts with a stilted politeness. She would be harder to win over than her children. But what she didn't understand was Seb had been raised with that level of indifference and even outright hostility. It didn't touch him.

What did concern him was the impact it was having on Agnesse.

Her sister and brother chatted and sparred in dizzying changes of direction until Mathilde reined them in, scolding both her younger children. For Isobel and Carl it seemed to have no impact; they carried on as before. For his future wife, even though they were not directed at her, he saw the admonishments landed a small blow each time. On the surface she appeared serene, but Seb sensed that beneath that calm surface each rebuke or correction increased her unease.

He didn't doubt Mathilde loved her daughter, but Agnesse was young and had not long ago become queen. Was her mother inadvertently putting undue pressure on her? If his future wife needed protecting from her mother, too, so be it. He'd not hesitate to step in if necessary.

He woke early and took the opportunity to walk part of the terrace below his suite. As with his arrival yesterday a soft mist lay about the grounds, but the palace itself was visible to him.

It spoke of generations of power and wealth enough to create comfort and grandeur all at the same time. In many ways it would be an easy place to call home. Who would not be soothed by its grace and beauty?

It was a long way from the hulking fortress he'd been raised in. So much softer, gentler.

However, judging by his future mother-in-law's behaviour yesterday, would he be any more welcome here than he had been by his own so-called family?

It made no difference. He'd have to get on with it. He may not have wanted a royal life and, if his family's beliefs had been any indication, it didn't particularly want him. Apart from Leo, who'd ever thought him capable of a role in the public eye?

Didn't mean he didn't know how to behave in one. He would carve a path somehow.

He'd worked privately with his chosen charities before. Supporting them with his time in person. Privately raising funds. He could do similar here.

He'd also stood in for Leo at social functions. Though never official ones.

He'd gone through women so he never had to test the limits of their affections. What if they were like his family underneath? Mercenary, obsessed with his status and not caring about the human being behind it.

And he adopted the persona of the playboy so he would never have to test the limits of the people's affections, either. Never try to win their respect and never be disappointed.

He turned away from the peace of the early morning, striding back in the direction of his rooms. His best man was due to arrive within the hour. Two hours after that they'd both be waiting in the chapel for the arrival of the bride. His days of sitting on the fence were over. He had to make a choice now.

The palace PR team had already written the press release that would announce the marriage of the queen. No mention was to be made of the pregnancy; only the immediate family knew about that. Instead, the union was to look like the result of an irresistible love match. The period of official mourning precluding any undue celebrations, they had the perfect excuse for a quick and low-key wedding.

A single photographer and journalist had been summoned to document the wedding celebrations, such as they were. All Agnesse would have to do was look happy and pretend that she'd married for love. She could gaze at Seb as if she wanted him. That was easy. Because, Heaven help her, she did. She wanted the comfort of his touch, a sign that they might have the chance at being a proper family. She wasn't ready to give up on that dream just yet.

Last night, as they were about to go to their separate rooms, she'd blurted that he could stay with her.

He'd declined.

'I think we should respect tradition and not see each other until we meet in the chapel. And an early night might be beneficial.' He glanced down to her still-flat belly. 'It's not just you to consider now.' Then the corner of his mouth had lifted in an ironic smile. 'As for me, the delights of the Rose suite await.'

She'd longed for the reassurance of his touch, but he'd not so much as taken her hand, just bowed, clicked his heels, and left her, calmly walking away while she was a churning mess of unrequited longing.

Her mother and Dorel had arranged a selection of suits and dresses for Agnesse to try. She'd opted for an elegant ivory silk two-piece. It's fitted jacket hugged her still-slim waist; a peplum fell to her hip. The straight skirt finished just below her knees, demure, but elegant and showing off a hint of tanned leg. But peeking out along the jacket lapel and skirt hem was a trim of ivory Guipure lace. A nod to her bridal state without being too ostentatious. Her hair was caught up in an elegant side chignon. Topped by a veiled ivory pillbox hat.

Her mother fussed at it.

'I'd so looked forward to your wedding one day. But that man, *that man*, has robbed us of it all.'

'He didn't get me pregnant on his own. I was

there, too,' Agnesse said. She wouldn't tell her that
Seb had been the one to call a halt until they had
protection and she'd admit to no one that they'd
have not been in this position at all if she hadn't
seduced him. 'He's not to blame.'

'Of course he is. He can't help himself. He sees a
beautiful woman and he has to have her. However
beyond his status she may be.'

'He's a prince of Grimentz, Mama.'

'Only just. And who was his mother? The secretary. A nobody. Snaring herself an unwary royal.
Like mother, like son.'

'Mama!' Agnesse scolded. Her mother wasn't
normally a snob.

She looked shamefaced. 'I'm sorry. He's just not
what I'd hoped your husband would be like. I'd so
hoped you'd love each other.'

Agnesse swallowed the pain of that truth as best
she could. Even though she knew from the start he
could not offer her love, it still hurt that her mother
could see it. He didn't love her.

She tried not to focus on that, turning instead to
slip on the shoes Dorel had found. A pair of gorgeous, sky-high stilettos in ivory silk with a line of
Swarovski crystals running up the heels and onto
the shoe itself. Agnesse adored them and here was
a little bling to match the diamond-and-sapphire
ring Seb had presented to her at dinner last night.
When she'd looked up at him in surprise, he'd done
that little shrug again.

'I may not have many possessions but that's by choice. I didn't say I wasn't rich. I am. Rich enough to buy you as many baubles as your heart desires.'

She didn't want any more because this one was already quite perfect. Despite everything, her silly heart had skipped in delight. The sapphire matched her eyes; the surrounding tapered baguette diamonds gave the ring the look of a daisy.

Agnesse trembled. Soon, he'd add a matching gold band to her finger.

The only other adornment she wore were her pearl studs and her gold mourning medal. As would Seb. He was joining the Toivonens and would be required to mourn a man he'd never met. For today only she and her family would swap the black ribbon for one of pale grey.

She felt that her father would have approved of her new husband. Her mother couldn't see beyond his scandalous past. But her father would have seen the man behind the apparent indolence, to the intelligence and compassion that she was beginning to see in him. Perhaps that would be enough for their life together. Mutual respect.

She picked up her posy of daisies and meadowsweet. At her request, the wildflowers had been gathered from the meadows surrounding her father's mausoleum. A bee drawn by the promise of nectar flew in through the open window and settled on a daisy.

It was a much-needed symbol of good fortune

on a day that should have been full of celebration. She took her mother's arm, and the dowager queen smiled at her when she knew both of them wished her papa was there to walk her down the aisle.

She gave her mother a hug and headed for the door.

Generations of Toivonens had worshipped in this chapel. Been baptised, wed, or dispatched on their final journey to everlasting rest. They were high-born, every one of them, and yet, despite the vaulted ceilings, the elaborate carving of the dark wood pews and chandeliers overhead, the interior of this hallowed space felt humble. As the monarch who'd built it had intended. He'd been a devout man and wanted the simple whitewashed walls to be a sharp contrast to the gilded stucco of the palace state-rooms. An earthly reminder of the peace awaiting him in Heaven.

Waiting at the altar now, Seb would have pre-ferred something grander and more anonymous. This intimate family space was making him want to run like hell away from it all. Did the archbishop pick up on his turmoil? He chose that moment to give him a reassuring nod.

Seb stared resolutely ahead.

But the daisy boutonnières that he and Leo had been given to wear glowed in his peripheral vi-sion. The scent of them, and the riot of roses and hedgerow greenery adorning the altar, mingled in the air. A fresh, vivid scent that Seb suspected he'd remember forever.

Behind him, at the rear of the chapel, Isobel and Carl whispered together like excited teenagers. But otherwise, the pews were empty. This was to be a perfunctory affair. No extended family, no other guests. It added uncomfortably to the feeling of intimacy. This time it was Leo who picked up on the fresh jangle of nerves and clapped a reassuring hand to Seb's shoulder.

Seb tugged at his collar. Not that it was needed. He was impeccably dressed in a charcoal suit and ice-blue tie. His best man similarly attired.

The chapel could be reached from inside the palace, but that entrance remained closed. Instead, his bride had elected to walk to her wedding through the morning sunshine. And behind Seb, at the rear of the chapel, the great oak doors stood open with a view to the late king's summer meadows beyond.

The archbishop cleared his throat and Seb finally turned to look back down the nave. He heard Leo's sharp intake of breath.

Seb wasn't sure he'd be able to breathe at all.

Silhouetted in the great stone arch of the doorway stood his bride. She waited until Isobel and Carl fell in behind her, then on her mother's arm, the Queen of Ellamaa advanced towards him.

Outside the chapel there was an elm tree; a breeze set its leaves fluttering and the light pouring through the stained-glass windows became a dancing kaleidoscope of green and gold. As Agnesse moved through it her beauty was almost unearthly, like she belonged more to the next world than this.

And yet, she carried his child.

Seb's mouth went dry. How could he protect such an ethereal creature when he was just a man, with feet of clay? The terror threatened to claw through his chest.

Would she be safe? Please God, let her be safe.

Her ivory suit revealed only a hint of neckline and the lower part of her tanned legs. But that modesty was deceptive. The suit hugged her figure, emphasising her lush curves, her breasts, the flare of her hips. It heated Seb's blood.

His heart pounded as she arrived beside him and Mathilde symbolically presented her daughter's hand to the groom. He closed his own around it, like a priceless gift he must treasure. But her veil hid her eyes from him. He desperately wanted to push it aside so he could see her expression, to be reassured that she was real.

Of course she was real: her fingers trembled.

Or was the tremor in his?

He hadn't expected this, to be so moved by his bride. He closed his heart to it. It would serve no purpose. She needed him to be strong for her and their unborn child, not behave like a lust-struck fool. Because surely that was all it was—lust.

He wouldn't allow it to be anything else.

They turned as one to face the altar.

Beside her stood the Dowager Queen of Ellamaa. Beside him, the Crown Prince of Grimentz, both there to bear incontrovertible and unassailable royal witness; there would be no denying the validity of this marriage.

It might have been rapturously romantic had the groom not worn such a grim, dark expression and the woman beside him not been choking on her replies as if she could barely get them out.

But their eyes met, briefly, and hers flashed with a yearning that caught him off guard and somehow seared him to his soul.

Then it was done, rings exchanged and the register signed. Seb tucked her hand into his elbow and led his bride back down the nave towards the sunshine.

The photographs were to be a cursory affair. Like the service. There to simply get the job done. They would be disseminated through the press this afternoon. One interview had been organised for after the wedding breakfast so the couple could announce their nuptials to the world.

Watching his bride's pale face, the way she clung to his arm, convinced Seb that he would be taking the lead in that interview and he would insist they keep it short. They wouldn't be announcing Agnesse's pregnancy anytime soon; another two months at least. After the first scan. But she was a monarch of only nine months standing and still on a steep learning curve. He could legitimately step in protectively at this stage. She might have nearly fainted when she'd discovered she was pregnant, but there'd been no more panic attacks that he knew of. The arrogant alpha in him preened. Was his presence protecting her from those, too?

He could be the one to spout some nonsense about them falling in love; he could make it sound convincing, make it *look* convincing for the photos.

That his wife, and, since he'd officially joined the Toivonen family, also his queen, could deliver the same impression, he was not so certain.

Wife.

Pregnant wife.

Could his lifelong fears, his nightmares, have become any more real? A spouse and an unborn child to protect from all that could go wrong for them.

Then Seb saw what awaited them outside.

The palace staff had gathered, forming an impromptu honour guard along the route he and Agnesse were to take back into the palace. He'd been the focus of the public gaze before; of course he had. Countless times. He was used to it. But not like this.

Whether he took the title of consort or not, here, in the small, intimate world of the Summer Palace, he was their prince. Husband to their queen and, not that they knew it yet, father to their unborn heir. He had no playbook for this. In Grimentz the people knew him for what he pretended to be, the pleasure seeker. They had no expectations of him beyond that. But here they were looking at him with genuine regard. What happened when they discovered he wasn't worthy of it?

He nearly tripped down the final step from the church to the flagstones beyond.

So it was Agnesse who summoned the smiles, stopping to chat with a footman, or the cook and her sous-chefs. Sharing a joke with a gardener. Graciously accepting all their good wishes while he walked stiffly beside her, wearing who knew what kind of expression on his face.

Behind him he heard Mathilde and Leo similarly working their way along the line. Even Isobel and Carl were doing their duty.

A young housemaid curtsied to him.

'Congratulations, sir, and welcome to Ellamaa.'

Seb might have muttered an acknowledgment. He doubted it had been that polite. Agnesse made a quip about them both being nervous, which raised a chuckle, saved the day, and they moved on.

He was experiencing emotions he didn't know how to deal with. Things he hadn't expected to feel. About Agnesse, about their baby. About the people of Ellamaa. A desire to be everything they needed him to be. His father would have laughed in his face at that.

Let others see the real you, Agnesse had said.

Impossible.

'Come on, brother, hurry up. We're starving.'

Isobel and Carl sped past him, leaping up the steps

and through the French windows into the palace, disappearing from view. Precisely what he wished he could do right now.

But perhaps he could. If he pushed this emotionally stunted creature aside and turned to the old, familiar Seb.

The staff began to disperse, returning to their duties. The photographer was ready, snapping informal shots as he waited for the royal newlyweds.

Seb took Agnesse's hand and with a practised smile, raised it to his lips.

'You are more lovely than I can say, *ma chérie*.'

And if her beautiful face suddenly clouded over, well, he wouldn't let that bother him. She thought she saw right through his mask to the real Seb. Maybe she did. But he needed that mask right now. He'd promised her the protection of a husband and father for their child, nothing more. Certainly nothing deeper…

So that mask was staying firmly in place.

He posed for the photographs. Gazed feelingly into his bride's eyes. Kissed her and felt her lips trembling as they clung to his, but once that image had been captured, he pulled away. Convincing himself that he felt nothing. It was just the emotion of the day.

Then he smiled as he stood amongst his new family. He chatted pleasantly with the archbishop and politely with his mother-in-law. Sampled the delicacies laid out for the wedding breakfast, sipped champagne and fielded the teasing of his new brother-in-law and sister-in-law. Everything, in fact, that could possibly be expected of a bridegroom.

Except for the minimal attentions he paid to his bride. All the time, from the corner of his eye, he could see Agnesse watching him, her blue eyes bruised with hurt and confusion.

An hour later it was time for Leo to leave.

'Walk me to my car?' his cousin asked.

They strolled together through the gardens, heading to the forecourt where a limo waited.

'I thought the marriage service was rather beautiful,' Leo said. 'Very moving in its simplicity.'

Seb said nothing.

'And that was a genuinely touching gesture by the staff.' He paused to acknowledge the greeting of a passing gardener. 'But then the Ellamaese have always had great affection for their royal family.'

Seb made a noncommittal grunt.

Leo halted by a rose bush that was covered in lush scarlet blooms. He bent to sniff one. 'Lovely. The grounds here are exceptionally pleasant.' He glanced back over his shoulder. 'As is the palace. There are definitely worse places you could call home.'

Right now Seb couldn't think of many. Moving services, touching gestures, great *affection*. All of that scared the hell out of him and yet, here he was, helplessly trapped in the middle of it.

'Your mother-in-law might be a harder nut to

crack but I've no doubt you'll charm her in the end.'
Leo smiled. 'She'll eventually realise what a catch
her daughter has made.'

Seb's feet scraped angrily across the crushed
gravel path as he swivelled to glare at his cousin.
'Okay, spit it out. Whatever it is you're trying to
say with all this nonsense give it to me straight.'

Leo studied him, his head tipped to one side.

'Just that I think you've chosen well. It could be
a good life for you. If you're open to it.'

'I'll do what I did in Grimentz. What I've always
done—my duty. But there can be nothing more.
And you of all people should know exactly *why*
that is.' Neither of them had fared well under the
parenting of their respective fathers.

'I'm just saying maybe it's time to try a different
way?' His solicitous tone set Seb's teeth on edge.

'No.'

'Agnesse has feelings for you. You know that,
right?' Leo said.

Seb's chest tightened. His moments of weakness
in the chapel came back at him. Feelings he hadn't
known he could feel. If she did, it made no difference. He was only here to keep her and their child
safe. He hardened the heart he didn't even know
he had.

'If that's true I'm sorry for it. You know me. I
can't return any of it.'

A mother he'd never had the chance to love, and

a father who'd withheld all affection. How could their son know how to give anything of himself?

Leo searched his face, a scrutiny that Seb bore calmly. If his cousin was looking for anything there to refute that claim, he'd find nothing. Except that maybe he thought he had because Leo's eyes narrowed on him. 'Trust me. I really wouldn't be so sure of that.'

Seb was.

As Leo drove away, Seb knew he'd never been surer of anything in his life. He had to be.

If his experiences that morning had been anything to go by, his very survival here depended on it.

CHAPTER TEN

'I'LL BE HONEST, MA'AM. The prince has rather surprised me.'

The archbishop was on his second glass of champagne. Agnesse was still pretending to sip her first. Avoiding it would have been a dead giveaway and she was certain he already had his suspicions after the request for a special licence and the haste of their wedding.

'I really wasn't expecting such a serious-minded young man,' he continued. 'He asked me about the state of our mental health charities. He gave me quite a grilling.' The archbishop chuckled. 'Good job I was up on the facts. He seemed so interested I've agreed to make an introduction or two for him.'

Agnesse's heart swelled. Seb, her *husband*—that was going to take some getting used to—was a good man and she could only be glad that others were recognising that.

Sadly, the dowager queen wasn't currently one of them. 'I'm glad he's intending to do something useful with all his free time,' she said, tartly. 'Did he tell you he's refusing the position of official consort?'

The archbishop nodded. 'He mentioned he intends to live as a private citizen.'

Her mother sniffed. 'Perhaps he should have thought of that before he…he…'

Agnesse silently filled in the blanks: *impregnated my daughter*?

'Before he proposed to Agnesse,' her mother said with a sneer in his direction as her despised son-in-law returned to the salon.

Agnesse felt a warning constriction in her chest. She didn't want to be caught between loyalty to her mother and loyalty to her husband, but if her marriage was to have any chance at all, she would have to choose sides, and she would have to choose Seb's.

The nausea that had fortunately held off that morning arrived now. Whether it was from panic or pregnancy hormones she couldn't tell. Nor did she care. She felt utterly miserable and needed this day to end.

As he moved towards her, she sensed that Seb had spotted her distress at once. Even though there'd been that sudden emotional withdrawal as they'd left the chapel, there was a concern in his gaze now.

'Your Majesties, Your Grace.' He took Agnesse's hand. 'My bride is looking tired. If you would excuse us, I think she should rest.'

The archbishop blustered, 'Why, of course, yes, you're a young couple and it's a wedding.' As if in the simplicity of the celebrations he'd quite forgotten the purpose of his presence here today. Agnesse wished she could, too. Suddenly, the thought of being alone with this coolly detached Seb was unnerving.

The archbishop made his farewells but as Seb led his wife away, her mother joined them. 'I need a moment of your time, Sebastien,' she said, falling in step beside them.

'Of course,' he said with a curt nod. They walked together in an uncomfortable silence. Agnesse caught in the middle of the hostility emanating from her mother and a brooding irritation from Seb.

'I wanted to give you this,' her mother said, presenting Seb with an envelope as soon as they crossed the threshold of Agnesse's suite. However much she wished it, Agnesse knew that was no wedding gift her mother had just handed over.

'As you are choosing not to take on any official role…' Could her mother have sounded any more disapproving? 'I feel it's important we lay down some ground rules for you, Sebastien.'

Agnesse winced. What ground rules? The moment they'd left the chapel it had felt as if the real Seb had withdrawn behind an invisible barrier. She didn't need any additional *rules* getting in the way, too.

'I've had a list drawn up of palace protocols and how you'll be expected to behave,' the dowager queen explained. 'I've no idea about the informalities allowed in Grimentz but here you will, of course, only ever address my daughter as ma'am or Your Majesty whenever you are in company together.'

Agnesse sank onto a seat. She couldn't bear it. Perhaps stuffy protocol decreed it, but that wasn't what she wanted. She and Seb were equals.

'Thank you, Your Majesty.' Seb pocketed the envelope without even glancing at it, then crossed to the door and held it open for her mother. 'But have no fear that I'll disgrace the palace. I assure you, I've been most thoroughly tutored in the niceties of royal hierarchies and court behaviours.'

Agnesse heard the lifetime of bitterness heaped into that statement and remembered Seb's comments about unkind fathers. Was that a glimpse into what he'd meant? Had his tutoring been harsh?

'And now if you'll excuse us. My wife and I would like some time alone together.'

Her mother's mouth fell open at being so summarily dismissed. For a moment Agnesse thought she might refuse to leave, but perhaps something in the unblinking gaze of her new son-in-law persuaded her that this was a battle she'd lose.

As she stepped over the threshold Seb added, 'From now on I would ask that you respect our privacy and only enter our suite when invited.'

'But Agnesse is my daughter.'

Despite her distress Agnesse stifled a wry smile. *Careful, Mother, that was dangerously close to shrill.*

'But now she's married. Her circumstances have changed and so must your expectations. Good day, Your Majesty.'

As he closed the door on her mother's palpable shock, Agnesse slumped in relief. Seb had stood in her corner. He'd seen her visibly crumbling before her mother's overbearing behaviour and he'd stepped in. Her mother meant well; she knew it. Like all of them, she was struggling to make sense of the world without her beloved husband in it and sometimes she misjudged, like just now.

On the sideboard sat a drinks tray. Seb went to it, filled a glass, and brought it to her.

'Still water. One cube of ice, one slice of lime.'

She looked up at him in surprise. 'I pay attention,' he said. 'I did think of adding an extra ice cube and a lemon slice but perhaps one act of rebellion is enough for you today.' He wasn't smiling exactly but there was a warmth in his eyes that seeped into her heart and took away some of the chill, nevertheless.

Agnesse took the water from him, wrapping her fingers around the cool glass. The nausea was receding. 'I know my mother loves me and only wants what's best for me.'

'But right now she can't see past the scandalous man you've installed in the palace. It was never what she intended for you. Give her time. She'll adjust.'

How was he being so reasonable after her mother's insulting behaviour? Was this yet another surprising facet to Seb?

'She never used to be like this. Since I became

queen, she's been so exacting and critical. I know she's grieving and is determined for me to succeed. For me and for Papa's memory.'

'Have you told her about the panic attacks?'

Agnesse shook her head.

'Then perhaps you should. Imagine all the support she must have given to your father over the years. All the knowledge she has. She could help you.'

She couldn't bear the thought of admitting she was having problems to anyone else. It would make it real. Her father had always had so much belief in her. She couldn't let him down.

'I'm sure they'll go away soon, and I don't want to worry her. It's my job to be strong for *her*. I'm queen now.'

He took her chin and tipped her face upward. 'And when did the queen last eat, hmm? You touched nothing of the wedding breakfast.' The warmth of his hand was so welcome she would have leant into it, but he'd already withdrawn it. As if he didn't want the contact any longer than necessary.

'Last night. I couldn't face a thing this morning.'

'The sickness again?' he asked gently.

This care for her was so irresistible. In the absence of anything else more intimate she'd grasp it. She smiled at him. 'Just nerves, I think.'

'In that case you must eat.' He called for Dorel and ordered a tray be sent up for the queen.

'Anything in particular, sir?'

'Whatever you think may tempt her.'

Agnesse's gaze flickered over her husband: to the broad shoulders and long legs; to the strong jaw with its faint bruise, which Dorel, the magician that she was, had disguised with concealer for the wedding photographs; and to his wickedly sensuous mouth that haunted her dreams.

She didn't want food. She wanted him, crushing her in his arms. Pressing her to the nearest available flat surface. Spreading her thighs—

'You look a little flushed.' Frowning, he placed the back of his hand to her forehead. 'Would you like to lie down?'

Yes, with you on top of me and both of us stripped naked.

As this didn't seem to be an option, she went to the bathroom to splash cool water on her face.

A collection of male toiletries had appeared on the vanity unit. Amongst them a razor, a shaving brush, and wooden bowl containing a puck of shaving soap. She picked it up and the scent of sandalwood wafted towards her.

She brought it closer to her nose and breathed in. A needy inhalation that delivered as much of that scent as possible. She couldn't get enough of that smell. It was practically the essence of Seb.

While her own favourite perfume now turned her stomach, the smell of her baby's father had apparently become irresistible.

But what were his things doing in here? She'd

had the palace team prepare the suite of rooms along the hallway, connected to hers by a door in their respective dressing rooms. She hadn't for a moment thought he'd want to *share* her rooms. She wasn't sure how she felt about it, if she was ready for that level of familiarity when the man didn't even seem to want to touch her.

She stalked back into the lounge, where he'd seated himself on her sofa and was scanning her mother's cursed list.

'What's this?'

He studied the little wooden bowl she held up. 'Shaving soap,' he said. 'My favourite brand. You might want to take note for Christmas and birthdays.'

'No, what's it doing in my bathroom—?'

'*Our* bathroom,' he said.

She remembered now, when he'd expelled her mother, he'd said *our* suite and she'd been too distracted to notice.

'You're planning to be in my rooms, not your own down the hall?'

'My duty is here so where else would I be?' For a moment he wore that same hunted expression he'd had when they'd left the chapel and saw the palace staff lined up to congratulate them. As if the responsibility terrified him.

She'd have challenged him on that, too, but the tray of food arrived. And he made her sit and hovered over her until she'd tried a little of everything and was satisfied she'd eaten enough. And then he asked if she wanted to lie down and rest now.

Like she was an invalid. Not a bride.

She could have suggested he lie down with her, but this coolly detached man felt distant and unapproachable. She'd rather spare herself the embarrassment of being rebuffed.

'I'm not tired. Perhaps we could use this time to get to know one another better.'

'Yes, of course,' he said, looking hunted again. For a moment it felt like she'd trapped a part-tame bear and the wildness in him was desperate for a way out.

'The archbishop said you'd asked about the mental health charities in Ellamaa?'

Seb's jaw tightened and he gave the briefest of nods.

'That night in Vienna you mentioned you work with one,' she said.

'I did. It's an important cause to support.'

'Do you do a lot of that? Supporting good causes?'

This time she thought he wasn't going to answer at all. He looked so closed off. But then he sank into the sofa beside her. 'I donate a considerable sum to good causes every year.'

Well, that was unexpected. 'Considerable?'

'Hundreds of millions.'

Her jaw fell open. 'Of your own income?'

He helped himself to a plump strawberry from the bowl of berries on her tray. 'Not exactly. I raise the money by investing and then donate the bulk of the profits to the charities I like to support.'

'You mean you have people manage your investments for you?'

He snorted as if she'd insulted him. 'I have a small team for admin purposes, but I've always done the bulk of research myself. It's my job, Agnesse. It's what I—' he sketched out inverted commas with his fingers '—do with my time.'

Her mother would be astonished by that, and rightly so. Agnesse was rather impressed herself.

'And how long have you been investing?'

He collected another strawberry. As his lips closed around it, Agnesse shivered in remembered delight of when he closed that mouth around the tips of her breasts.

'I started when I was sixteen.'

'*Sixteen?* You were just a boy.'

'But old enough to know I needed to find something to do with my life.'

Agnesse sensed he wasn't being entirely truthful. That the sixteen-year-old Seb had more compelling reasons for his financial planning. Why would a boy born into wealth and royalty need an escape? Unkind father, perhaps?

'You wanted to be financially independent of you family.'

His green eyes flashed. 'Yes,' he said emphatically. Well, that was an honest reaction at least. 'And I'd have gone as far away as I could. But I couldn't leave Leo. He's always been like a brother to me. I owe him.'

'So you stayed out of duty.'

'Of course, out of duty.'

Not love, then. The same reason he'd married her. Her heart deflated a little.

'Are the von Frohburgs really so terrible?'

'Not Leo and Max. But the rest of them are, and they hate me because my mother wasn't one of them.'

'Will you tell me about her?'

'I never knew her. She died giving birth to me.'

Agnesse wanted to reach out and take his hand but didn't think he'd want that sort of intimacy.

'But I have a photograph.' He dug his phone from his pocket and leant forward, elbows propped on his thighs, as he scrolled through images.

He handed her the phone.

'When my father died, they found two photographs tucked away amongst his possessions. This is one of them.'

A young woman, heavily pregnant, sat at a piano. She smiled up at the camera. Had it been taken by Seb's father? The image had a touching intimacy to it. And tragedy, too. Short weeks after it had been taken, she would be dead.

'Fabienne Bonfils. My mother,' he said.

'She was beautiful. She looks happy, too. And young.'

'She was younger than you are now when she died,' he said with a pained glance to Agnesse. This might account for the look of sheer terror she'd seen in his face today. Perhaps she could understand that. He might be worried history would repeat itself.

'You said there were two photographs.'

A host of emotions went to war in his green eyes. Whatever triumphed, it secured his decision to show her the next image. Fabienne again, but this time joined by a man.

'It's your parents.'

Of course it was. Who else could it be? The man beside her bore such a striking resemblance to them both. His father's chin and nose, his mother's eyes.

Fabienne sat smiling in the arms of Prince Georg, whose gaze was filled with love. His hand spread protectively over her rounded belly. Seb studied the image with her in silence until she looked up at him.

'It's a lovely picture but you didn't really want to show me, did you?' Agnesse said.

He ran a hand across his face. 'I have a complicated relationship with that photograph,' he said at last. 'My father's first wife came from one of the best European families. She brought wealth and good connections. The von Frohburgs have always been obsessed about protecting the bloodlines,' he said, bitterly. 'Fabienne was his secretary. She brought nothing but a pretty face, and if that photo is anything to go by, a genuine love for my father. It must have been a revelation for him. His first marriage was arranged. And not happy. My half brother remembers them fighting. By the time this photo was taken they'd been divorced for two years. It had been an ugly and bruising process. My father was not supported by the family. And then this pretty young thing arrives in the midst of that cold, love-less life and you can see it lit him up inside.'

Agnesse *could* see it. The wonder and joy in Prince Georg's eyes.

'They do so look happy together,' Agnesse said.

'The von Frohburgs hated my mother from the start. So after their wedding they moved to France. But when my mother died, he seemed like he lost all hope and went back to Grimentz, and I was raised there with Leo and Max.'

'Did your father ever speak of her to you?'

He gave a bark of bitter laughter. 'My father rarely spoke to me, full stop. I never got the chance to know anything about her from him. What little I know I've had to piece together myself. She had no family so there weren't even any grandparents or siblings I could talk to about her. She's like a ghost.' There was such loss in that statement, in-stinctively Agnesse reached out and placed her hand on his arm. He didn't shake it off and instead, sent her a tight smile.

Her own mother could be trying but she was there; Agnesse had at least known her and knew she was loved. By both her parents. She began to get some un-derstanding of what Seb had lost, what he had never had. The secure bond of a family. How much harder for him to see that picture of the three of them, his father embracing his young wife, his hand spread protectively over her full belly, over his unborn son. Before that family was cruelly ripped apart.

'I don't think he could ever forgive me. The rest of the extended family certainly couldn't. Materially, I wanted for nothing, but it was like he couldn't bear to look at me. I think all the life went out of him when he lost my mother. And I was no compensation. He saw me as the opposite. The reason he'd lost the only thing he'd ever truly loved.'

Then he shook himself. 'But that's enough sadness on our wedding day. Would you like to hear about the projects I've invested in?'

Seb had never shared that much about his life with anyone. He'd always thought the bitter emotional scars his father and family had inflicted on him were better left unexplored. But sharing those details with Agnesse, seeing her smile down at his mother's image, had brought him an odd kind of solace.

It made him realise, too, that he should share more details of himself. At the very least, his new wife should know she hadn't married a wastrel, that he was a man of substance and more than just his playboy image. He owed her that, surely?

So they talked, and she'd begun to relax. And the day ahead progressed and turned to evening.

He'd discarded his jacket and tie. Her jacket was gone, too, revealing a silk camisole that clung to her breasts and was leaving little to his imagination. Not that he needed to use it. The utter perfection of her breasts had been imprinted in his mind since Vienna. Fuelling much erotic torment since that night.

She'd slipped off the sky-high, crystal heels he'd found so alluring—he knew he'd be having fantasies about her dressed in nothing but those.

She'd tucked her legs beneath her and scooted closer until she was leaning against him so she could point at the images he was bringing up on his phone.

'What's this one?'

'An artisan baker. It was one of my earliest investments. They still make the best sourdough you'll ever taste.'

He'd shown her other pictures. Other companies and initiatives he'd invested in. The latest project he'd supported was on a significantly bigger scale. A company developing hydrogen fuel technologies to heat homes and businesses with cleaner energy.

She'd sat back in laughing astonishment. 'The gossip columnists really have no idea, have they? You are nothing like the man they say.'

'Some of it's true,' he said with a glint in his eye, and she dimpled at him and his breath had caught. He could so easily have reached for her then, starting something that would have ended with them in bed together for a real wedding night.

But his mother's face haunted him. Younger even than Agnesse was now. Pregnant and so full of hope. Her death had blighted three lives. Not just his parents' but his own. He was cursed by the endless terror of losing someone he cared about.

He closed his mind to it. Tonight was not the time to think about it.

At some point she had fallen asleep propped on his shoulder. One minute they'd been talking and the next she couldn't keep her eyes open.

His beautiful bride who had secrets of her own.

He hoped she'd tell her mother about her panic attacks because he had no doubt that Mathilde would help. She was as devoted and protective as a pit bull. He and she weren't going to be friends anytime soon, but Seb couldn't fault her loyalty to her daughter. But he didn't care about her list of protocols. Nothing on it he hadn't had rammed down his throat when he was a boy. He didn't scare easily.

With the warmth of Agnesse at his shoulder and the steady rhythm of her soft breathing, he brought up his mother's photo again.

She looks so happy, Agnesse had said. He'd always thought that, too. Despite what happened next to her, it had given him great comfort to think she'd once been happy and well loved.

Seb scrolled through to that next photograph with his father gazing adoringly at his young wife.

The von Frohburgs never forgave his father, and by association, him, for marrying outside his social class. There'd been mutterings about Seb's legitimacy but fortunately he was the image of Prince Georg, except for the eyes. They were all his mother. Soft and beguiling, or so countless women had told him. Perhaps that was the reason his father had rejected his younger son. It was that or each day see the living, breathing reminder of all that he'd lost the day his wife had died.

A true von Frohburg had eyes of blue, chilly and aloof. His warm green eyes were another reason for them to snub him.

Agnesse made an adorable snuffling noise and settled again.

The thought of anything happening to her curled icy fingers in Seb's chest. This woman who at one moment could address a packed room with aplomb, and the next was fighting for breath on the floor of her bathroom.

Physical intimacy, taking a woman to bed, was easy. It was this emotional intimacy that he didn't know how to handle. He'd sought the connections he'd missed out on elsewhere in the only way he could. With endless women. But he gave his heart to no one, truly *shared* himself with no one.

Maybe it was just that she was easy to talk to. Maybe it was something to do with those blue eyes that seemed to see past the playboy prince to Seb, the real man behind it, but he'd *wanted* to share with Agnesse. And wasn't that a revelation?

But it was getting late, and she really should be in bed. A pregnant woman needed her rest.

She was so dead to the world she barely stirred when he gently lifted her in his arms and carried her to the bedroom. His bedroom, too, for the foresee-able future. She mumbled something at him when he slipped her out of the ivory skirt. She'd taken all the pins from her hair long ago and it lay in soft gold waves across her pillow. He stopped himself from running his fingers through it. He also left the camisole and panties on.

He'd vowed to himself he wouldn't touch her, and undressing her completely would have been a trial too far.

He pulled the sheet over her and she turned to her side and was deeply asleep again in moments.

Feeling like he'd had a lucky escape, Seb headed for his dressing room to ready himself for sleep.

Seb woke slowly and with an unexpected feeling of well-being. Like he'd slept the deep, untroubled sleep of the righteous. First surprise.

The second was that Agnesse was in his arms. Or rather, they were wrapped around one another, limbs entwined as if they'd found each other in the night and couldn't let go.

And right now he didn't mind.

She was soft and warm. He drifted back to sleep.

When he woke again he was alone, and from the bathroom came the sound of Agnesse retching.

'Go away,' she said, miserably, her voice echoing in the porcelain as he appeared in the doorway. Instead, he went to her, gathered up her hair and gently rubbed her spine as another bout of nausea hit.

At last, she slumped backwards and propped herself against the wall.

'All done?' he asked.

'For now, I think.'

He dampened a flannel and handed it to her.

'Is this going to be a thing for us?' she asked. 'You rescuing me from the bathroom floor?'

'It's what I signed up for yesterday. For better or worse, remember?'

'You probably weren't expecting it to be *worse* so soon in the marriage. Some honeymoon this is going to be.' She swiped the flannel back and forth over her mouth. She'd hastily pulled on a wrap; it was knotted haphazardly. Her hair in disarray. And yet, had she ever looked lovelier to him?

He told her so.

She snorted and stared at him like he'd become a simpleton.

He took the flannel from her and helped her to her feet. 'Anyway, I thought we weren't having a honeymoon,' he said.

'Just as well if I'm going to vomit all through it.'

Suddenly, yesterday's terror uncoiled and slithered through his gut. 'This is normal, isn't it? Perhaps we should speak to the doctor later, to be certain?'

'Relax. It's horrible but perfectly normal. I'll be better after a shower and a coffee. Give me fifteen minutes to do some repair work because, despite what you think, I don't feel lovely. That was a sweet thing to say, by the way,' she said, shooing him out of the bathroom. 'Sweet, but deranged.'

But when Agnesse emerged from the shower it wasn't to her usual cafetière of coffee. It was to a table for two set by a sunny window. Seb occupied one of the seats. In front of the other, a place had been set with breakfast things.

No coffee, she noted. But a teapot and toast rack with two dainty triangles of white bread with the crusts neatly removed.

'I didn't order this.'

'No, I did,' he said pleasantly. 'I understand eating breakfast can often help with the queasiness.'

'But I just want coffee. I never eat breakfast.'

'As you're pregnant, how about you start now?'

Dressed in nothing but navy silk pyjama bottoms, the sun beating down on his sculpted torso, he looked practically edible. *How about I eat you for breakfast?* she thought.

Last night they'd talked and she started to understand her husband a little more. His courage and determination to forge a new life for himself and help others along the way was impressive and deeply moving.

She could have talked to him all night.

But embarrassingly, she'd fallen asleep. Just like that. Perhaps that was the baby hormones, too. She felt another bout of nausea coming on.

She didn't even remember getting into bed last

night. Certainly not taking off her skirt. She'd woken in her underwear, sprawled over Seb's chest, her leg thrown over his thighs. As she carefully lifted herself off him, she was relieved he hadn't woken. She'd have had to apologise to him for being plastered all over him when he'd made it clear he didn't want that from her.

Last night he hadn't made any kind of move on her. He'd slept in her bed all night and hadn't touched her.

Duty, that was why he was here. Nothing more. Just like he'd done for Leo. She'd do well to remember that.

Now he gestured to the seat beside him. 'Agnesse, you need to eat something. Please.'

He'd delivered that plea with a flash of his green eyes, and she found her feet obeying him. She sank into the empty seat. If this had been a real honeymoon she'd have perched herself in his lap and teasingly fed that toast to him instead.

On a sigh of frustration, she picked up the first slice of toast and nibbled carefully. Surprisingly, her stomach didn't rebel. She tried another bite.

Seb poured the tisane into a cup and made a point of edging that towards her, too.

'It's ginger tea. Midwives swear by it for morning sickness.'

'Aren't we the expert this morning?' She took a sip while he watched her with an expression she couldn't decipher.

'Happy now?' she said.

He blinked and that moment passed. His mouth curved into a lazy smile. 'I will be when you've finished that cup and both slices of toast.'

'Both?'

'It's hardly a banquet, Agnesse, and let's try it to see if it works, shall we?'

'I've married a tyrant,' she muttered. 'That's got to be sufficient grounds for an annulment. I might call my lawyers.'

'Please do,' he said, quite unperturbed by her bad temper. 'Just as soon as you've finished your breakfast. And if you are going to be such a ray of sunshine every morning, I might call my own.'

'Please do,' she said, shoving the second piece of toast into her mouth and chewing with a baleful glare in his direction.

But she was actually feeling better, thinking maybe the ginger tea and toast could work and feeling secretly touched by his efforts on her behalf.

And even more surprising after last night she felt the mask Seb had hidden behind yesterday had slipped, and she was getting a glimpse of the real man.

CHAPTER ELEVEN

THE DAYS PASSED and settled into a routine with a frustrating glimpse of an intimacy, of a loving relationship with her husband, that Agnesse could never quite grasp.

There was the tender care of her but also those moments when he allowed her to see the real Seb. Vulnerable, hurt, compassionate.

Oh, she wanted so much to see more of him. That man drew her in.

He would always take breakfast with her. Probably to satisfy himself that she had eaten. He was usually there for dinner with the family, too. But apart from a chaste kiss good-night, he barely touched her. She was burning up with frustration and hurt. Did he really not desire her?

If she couldn't have the emotional life with him that she craved, then she would get on with being the best queen she could be. It was the life she'd been born to live, after all. She would embrace it. She would *own* it. And she was damn well going to be good at it. Whatever the pressure. However long the to-do list that remained at the end of each day.

She met with ministers, opened hospitals, unveiled plaques, attended military parades. For none of these did Seb join her. Only on the less formal occasions, the visits to charities and organisations she supported. Then he was there, showing an interest and a surprising knowledge of the work being done at each, delighting everyone.

Her husband knew he could charm people. What he didn't understand was it happened when he wasn't even trying. It was him. There was something innately dazzling about him and people wanted to bask in it.

There were the appealing manners, the lazy smile, and for her alone, the quick but heated glances that never failed to send warmth to her belly. But there was more. There was, if you looked closely enough, a subtle vulnerability. Something guarded and fragile and perhaps not altogether under his control. Sometimes, when he thought he was unobserved, he would fold inwards and then it was like an injured bear had invaded her home and prowled its boundaries looking for an escape.

Mostly, he moved through the palace as if it hardly mattered who it belonged to. He had no need for it. But then even the walls seemed to sway closer as he passed, as if they yearned to hold him close for a moment. The palace might be Ellamaese, but now this foreign von Frohburg male had bewitched them all.

Her team was eager to please him. There were smiles, and greetings, and plans, and papers pressed into his hands for his consideration; completed tasks pointed out for his approval. She was happy that her people loved him. But whilst he was charm itself, not one of them really gained his absolute attention. Oh, none of them realised it. He managed to convey his complete focus on whomever had accosted him at that moment. But she knew that whenever she was close by his attention was on her.

Occasionally, she tested her theory. Lifting a languid hand to her brow and sighing faintly. And though he was apparently deep in conversation on the other side of the room, in the next instant he'd be beside her, his fingers lightly touching her shoulder. His green eyes full of concern.

It was irresistible, this attention. This care of her.

She felt herself falling more and more under its spell. Needing it, craving it. Like the palace staff looking for ways to draw him to her side and win a solicitous look, or better yet a smile.

Oh…the variety of smiles. The boyish one. The one filled with sexual promise that sent shivers of anticipation along her spine. And that beautiful but practised, distant one, where he went somewhere she was desperate to follow.

Emboldened one morning, she took his face between her palms and asked him outright what made him hide behind that mask. He'd closed off instantly, kissing her lightly and telling her she was imagining things. Why on earth did she think he needed a mask?

You tell me, she wanted to say, but wasn't brave enough because what if she discovered the dark truth that might lay in wait for her? That she wasn't actually that important to him and that was what he was hiding.

And then he might actually break her heart. What use would a broken woman be as queen, when what was needed was calmness, clarity, service? Where would be her strength? It would be in pieces, a tattered pile of unrequited need at the feet of this man.

All she had left by way of defence was work.

Agnesse grabbed it with both hands.

Her meeting in the city had gone well. She'd just secured extra funding for one of the youth organisations her father's charity supported. Now they could build a brand-new residential centre on an earmarked woodland site. Thousands of youngsters growing up in deprived areas would soon have the opportunity to experience all the benefits the countryside had to offer.

And the person she most wanted to tell was Seb. Last night she'd practised her speech on him, then he'd helped her revise it, and she knew it had been better because of it.

As she walked back to their suite music floated towards her down the corridor. Someone was playing her father's piano. No one had touched it since he'd passed away. Was it time for its regular tuning? There'd been no mention in her diary and Keert would have warned the family. It would be hard to hear the instrument that her papa had loved, and that had fallen silent with his death, being played again. She didn't recognise the piece, and the regular tuner rarely played more than chords anyway. The door to the music room was ajar. She peeked around it.

It was her husband seated at the piano, his fingers flying back and forth over the keyboard. So he was an accomplished pianist, too? As if she needed another reason to adore him.

She must have made a noise because his head swung towards her. The music stopped instantly.

'Hello.' He smiled and her heart swooped in recognition.

'Hello,' she answered, walking in.

'How was the meeting?'

'I got the funding.'

'Good girl,' he said with another lift of his lips. 'I knew you could do it.' Oh, she could bask in his praise all day. She dropped her bag and jacket on a chair.

'What were you playing just now? It was pretty but I didn't recognise it.' She drew closer and bent to kiss him. He may not be taking her to bed but he never refused her kisses so she gave them freely.

She noted the piano was bare of sheet music. He must have known that piece by heart.

'I think it was something my mother used to play.' He picked out a few notes with one hand. 'The music was found along with the photographs my father kept. I'd never heard it before but when

I began to play, it was so familiar. I wondered if I remembered it from when…'

'Your mother playing it while she was pregnant with you,' Agnesse said, gently finishing the thought that he could not.

'Yes.'

She heard all the longing in that brief reply. A yearning to find some piece of his mother, a connection to her when all chance of that had died with her. Her heart ached for him.

She sat beside him, placing her hand over her stomach. 'Perhaps our little blip might like to hear it, too. Would you play it again for us?'

Seb lifted her hand, pressed a kiss in her palm, then turned it over and placed it gently back over her abdomen. Heaven help her, but the man had all kinds of ways to melt a girl's heart.

He began to play. It was a bright, sweet, hopeful piece and he played it beautifully. Agnesse leant against his shoulder, mesmerised by his skilled fingers, and moved by the sadness of the story behind them.

When he finished she took his face in her hands and kissed him.

'That was lovely. You play well.'

'Leo, Max, and I all had lessons as boys. I was the only one who took to it. Once I saw that picture of my mother, I figured out why.'

He looked so lost for a moment that she kissed him again, but this time she sensed a shift in him.

An urgency that had been missing since they arrived here. Soon, it was he dictating the pace, his hands in her hair, holding her face to his. The brush of his lips becoming harder, more demanding.

She made a sound at the back of her throat. A call to passion. She'd wanted this from him so badly, and she prayed that he would not pull back from it as he generally did.

He answered that call, dragging his mouth from hers so he could feast on the sensitive skin of her neck. It wasn't enough for him. He popped a button on her blouse to get at more of her, then another and another until it was all but off. His panting breaths gusted hot into her hair as he reached behind her to drag it free.

Then they were on their feet, stumbling, banging blindly into the stole, bouncing off the side of the piano, until he braced against it to support them both.

She took advantage of their respective positions, unbuttoned his shirt, and ran her greedy hands across his chest. He groaned into her mouth helplessly. Oh, she liked that. She liked his weakness for her. She'd exploit it. It made her bold.

She stepped back from him, and never breaking eye contact, sank to her knees before him. With her hands she freed him. But it wasn't her hands she intended to pleasure him with.

The feel of him in her mouth was sublime.

She stretched her lips wide to accommodate the

girth of him. She teased the tip, the plump silken skin so soft beneath her tongue. Seb let out a fractured breath. An explosion of air, as if he'd been trying to stay in control and suddenly lost it.

She experimented with how deep she could take him. What the long, slow rasp of her tongue did to him as she sucked. A groan was wrenched from him this time. She smiled around him.

She reached up a hand and pressed a palm flat to his abdomen and she felt the tightening, the judder of powerful muscles as he fought to control himself. And she fought right back.

She took him deeper and watched his head drop back helplessly. His fingers clawed at the piano edge, his knuckles white. His gasps and moans filled the air. As sweet a music to her ears as the piece he'd played for her before. Perhaps sweeter, because she was the one wrenching those helpless sighs from him.

Her. The former Ice Queen. She felt thoroughly, gloriously, wanton now.

'Agnesse,' he said, brokenly, 'stop. I can't… I won't be able…'

Oh, you can and you will, she thought. And she wrapped her fingers around him, working at him, not letting up for a moment until he was beyond speech altogether. On a long, shuddering gasp he threw back his head and spilled into her mouth.

'Agnesse,' he breathed when he finally had the power to speak again. She loved how undone he was. How it made her feel so powerful. But now she had a problem.

Being a wanton was all very well—until you had to stand back up with your dignity still in place. Her skirt was tight. Her heels were high. There was no way she was getting to her feet without his help.

On a giggle she reached out to him so he could haul her to her feet. It was done but suddenly, she was beset with uncertainty. Was that any good for him? He seemed to enjoy it but that didn't mean she'd done it all right. She thought of all the women he'd been with. They'd have done *that* so many times before, they'd have known exactly what to do.

He leant in and suddenly, his mouth was on hers, in one of his swift, drugging kisses that could make a woman forget her own name.

'Stop overthinking it. It was good,' he said, a bewitching smile dancing at the edge of his lips. 'Perhaps I could return the favour?'

He scooped her up and carried her to one of the couches. He divested them both of the remainder of their clothes and lay her down, gazing at her body with absolute reverence.

'Do you have any idea how beautiful you are, *chérie*?' he said, placing his mouth just beneath her ear. Goose bumps flowered wherever his lips met her skin.

He trailed fingertips over her collarbone then lower, gliding between her breasts. He dipped his head, to kiss each nipple, then added the graze of teeth until both were puckered. He licked them then blew gently on the gleam of moisture. Agnesse moaned. He turned his mouth to her stomach, kissing it with reverence.

'Look away, precious blip,' he said to her still-flat belly. 'Your naughty papa is about to do some terribly wicked things to your beautiful mama.'

Agnesse squirmed with pleasure as he kissed all the way down her abdomen until his mouth was there. And his tongue. Hot and unbelievably exciting. Stroking and licking and sucking until she was a writhing ball of need. One leg was draped over the low back of the sofa. She still wore her shoes. Impossibly slender six-inch heels in burgundy suede. It felt so wanton again.

'I still have my shoes on,' she said when he paused long enough for her to catch her breath, or rather, for him to lift her left leg and drape it over his shoulder, the better to get at her.

'I've had so many fantasies about doing this to you, with you wearing nothing but your heels.'

She didn't get a chance to make any kind of coherent answer to that. His mouth was on her again and all she could do was gasp and moan.

Then he rose up, gathered her close, and slid into her. She was slick, so primed he was seated to the hilt in one move.

'Agnesse,' he sighed as breathless and needy as she was. *'Chérie.'*

He was caught up in this. Even if it was just sex,

it was still sex with her and she'd celebrate that a little.

He began to move. Slow, deep thrusts that came dangerously close to tipping her over the edge each time. But he played her body as he'd played her father's piano, with skill and gentle understanding, and coaxed such drawn-out delight from her that she trembled in his arms, and their shared bliss, when it came, was beyond anything she'd ever imagined.

Afterwards he seemed content to just hold her. Their limbs entwined, his fingers playing idly in her hair, her hand on his chest.

'I know you've felt neglected,' he said. 'But I was worried I might be too rough and hurt you or the baby.'

'You know our blip isn't even the size of a peanut yet. And pregnant women have sex all the time. Some of us actually *want* it all the time.'

She felt the rumble against her cheek as he chuckled. 'Then in the future I shall try to oblige, *ma chérie.*'

At last. She offered up a silent hallelujah to the universe. 'My hormones will thank you for it,' she said.

Eventually, they had to move. People would be wondering where they were. He helped her into her skirt and zipped it up. She found his shirt and buttoned him back into it, at least after peppering his broad chest with little kisses. He collected her jacket and bag in one hand and twined her fingers through his other.

'Right, *chérie*,' he said. 'It's time you were fed. Let's go freshen up, then and find you some dinner, shall we?'

Well loved, her hand safe in his, Agnesse could have almost believed she floated back to their rooms that evening.

On the terrace below their suite Agnesse saw Carl and her husband, deep in conversation. What about? she wondered.

They often talked this way now. Her brother she knew appreciated the presence of another male in the family. He missed their father and while no one could ever replace him, Seb was doing a sterling job of being a big brother.

As for Isobel, all the trouble she had once caused seemed long forgotten. Now her outrageous sister delighted in teasing and taunting the newest Toivonen family member. But he threw it all back in kind. It apparently pleased them both.

Even her mother, her disapproving, exacting mother, was mellowing, leaving some sheet music for him on the piano. When asked, she dismissed it as just an old piece she'd found lying around. But one morning Agnesse saw her standing outside the music room, the fingertips of one hand resting on the door, the other pressing a handkerchief to her mouth, as a piece her father used to play floated out from Seb's skillful fingers.

Agnesse quietly turned back the way she had come and left her mother with her memories. But she'd hugged that moment close. Her whole family had accepted him.

Then there was the sex; *oh, the sex*. It was everything she'd dreamed of, and more. Though he never said it, sometimes she even believed he was developing deeper feelings for her.

There'd been no more panic attacks. She was managing her workload, just. A second pair of hands—an official consort for example—would help enormously, but hey, a girl couldn't have everything.

Agnesse curled her hand over her abdomen. Even her little blip was behaving and her morning sickness was under control.

She had everything to look forward to. Life was good.

CHAPTER TWELVE

THE WOMAN WOULDN'T rest and it was driving him crazy.

She was trying to do too much. Her mother knew it, Keert knew it, the whole palace staff knew it, but his wife was refusing to see it.

He'd joined her in her study that morning so they could coordinate their diaries for the next month. He wasn't at her side for official duties. But social occasions were another matter and he often accompanied her on any charity visits. He enjoyed them. And people seemed to enjoy his presence. So far he was even getting favourable write-ups in the press. It was probably just the novelty of discovering that a playboy prince also had a caring heart.

The job was done and she'd closed the calendar on her screen and brought up her task list. Seb, standing at her shoulder as the list appeared, nearly ground his teeth at the sheer number of items on it.

No wonder she looked weary.

Although he knew in part he was responsible for that. She wasn't getting all the sleep she could. When they retired for the night, when she woke in his arms in the morning, they couldn't resist one another and the sex, quite frankly, was incredible.

Yes, he had made love to his wife—over and over—and the sky had not fallen.

The thought of it tightened his groin. He could banish the staff and take her over this desk right now. But after, he knew she'd go straight back to work.

She was already making so few concessions to being pregnant. At least she was taking breakfast now and the nausea had lessened. A small win in many fights he felt he needed to have. Back in Grimentz intervening would have been less problematic. He'd have told Leo he was worn out and needed to take a break. Not to be such a martyr and to get some rest.

That approach wouldn't run here. She'd be more likely to dig in her heels and work even harder. If that was possible.

'Your view to the gardens is impressive,' he said casually.

Without shifting her gaze from her computer screen, she said, 'It's one of the reasons I chose this room for my study.'

Really? Did she even look at them? he wondered.

'And how often do you actually get out there?'

'Out there?' Now she looked at the view for about five seconds. Then her attention was back on the screen again. 'Recently, hardly ever.'

'Seems such a shame. The guidebook waxes lyrical about the carp pond.'

Her head swung towards him in surprise. 'You read the guidebook?'

'I was hoping to impress you with my knowledge when you take me on the tour.' He sent her the crooked smile that he knew she found irresistible.

Even though he heard the hitch in her breathing, on this occasion the woman stubbornly resisted. 'You've just seen my diary. I really don't have the time.'

He stretched out a hand, gathering one of hers from the keyboard. 'Let's be spontaneous. It'll be fun. Surely, you can spare me a little time to help me settle in.'

'You've already been here a month. Isn't that sufficient settling-in time?'

He made a face at her. 'And yet, I'm still to see the much-vaunted carp pond.'

'Did you actually just pout at me?' she said, laughing.

Yes, he had. He wasn't beneath using underhanded tactics. It was his job to look after her and that included getting her to take some time off. So he'd gifted her with his best sexy pout. It did the trick. She got to her feet. Ten minutes later they were seated on the raised slabs that ran around the edge of the pond.

She sighed prettily. The first unrestrained sigh of contentment he'd heard from her outside the bedroom. 'I'd forgotten how lovely it is here,' she said.

His *lovely* wife was a vision in the sunshine. There were small changes to her body that he'd noticed. A fullness to her breasts, and they were more sensitive when he ministered to them at night. A slight thickening at her waist but no real baby bump yet. In just over a month, she'd have her first scan. He was a mix of excited and terrified. Would she be okay? Would their baby be okay?

She leant over to trail her fingers through the water. 'Would you like to hand-feed the fish?' she asked.

Seb was surprised. 'They'll let you do that?'

'My father trained them. Even though Papa is gone, his favourite fish, Gunter, still leads the others to this part of the pond. We could try.'

She beckoned to one of the gardeners working nearby. Minutes later there was a tub of fish food on the slabs between them and she was showing Seb what to do. Sure enough, with Gunter leading, the carp were soon swiping pellets from his fingers.

'Sometimes my father would bring me here. He'd talk about looking after the fish, but he was really talking about our country. I think he came out here to help him find different perspectives to a problem.'

'Or maybe,' Seb said, 'he just wanted to indulge in the pleasure of feeding his fish?'

Agnesse closed her eyes and tipped her face to the sun. She'd forgotten how restful this part of the garden was. No wonder her father had loved to come out here. This stretch of the garden bordered the wildflower meadows, and everywhere was alive with bees, the buzzing a drowsy soundtrack to the beat of warm sunshine.

She exhaled with a long, slow breath of contentment. When she opened them again, she met Sebastien's warm, knowing gaze. Oh, the sneaky, *sneaky* man.

'I've just been managed, haven't I?'

The corner of his mouth curved up into that crooked smile she adored.

'I did really want to see this pond. And I really wanted to see it with you.' He took her chin in his hand and drew her closer for a kiss. 'Thank you,' he said.

The gentle kiss to each cheek was all the more entrancing for being so chaste. Her eyes fluttered closed and Agnesse sighed, feeling more tension drain away from her. A bird trilled in a nearby bush; a breeze stirred through the grasses edging the walkway. Lavender and rose and Sebastien's sandalwood mingled in the air. And then there was the soft touch of his fingers caressing her cheek. She wanted to freeze this moment in time. The calm, quiet morning. The feeling, for the moment at least, of having nothing to do. The warmth and touch of Seb's fingers. Like he cared. Like this thing between them was real. Queen and consort. Husband and wife. The image was so irresistible to her, she spoke without thinking.

'You know I'd have more time for these sort of moments if you accepted the position of consort. We could share the workload.'

His fingers were instantly gone, and without opening her eyes she sensed the anger in him.

'I told you before we married that I didn't want that life. I'm supporting you in any way I can, but it will always be behind the scenes. No titles, no official role.'

'You attend social events and charities with me. How is that different?'

'No weight of expectation to live with,' he said, looking more grim and closed off than she had ever seen him. 'No judgemental family criticising your every move.'

He meant the von Frohburgs. But her family wasn't doing that. They'd embraced him; even her mother had warmed to him.

'You have a new family now,' she said, softly, wanting him to see it. He had her, and their baby when it came. Their own fledgling family. She could have everything she'd dreamed of. If only she could make him want it, too.

If only he wanted her.

'I'm doing my duty, Agnesse. I always will. That will have to be enough for you.'

'So you're content to let me work my fingers to the bone while you do *what*?'

She knew she was being unfair, but he was sitting there so calmly while she was getting more and more angry; it made her want to shove him backwards into that blasted pond.

'I work. You know this. I'm hardly idle all day while you slave to keep me housed and fed.' A muscle ticked in his jaw. Finally, she might be shaking that impenetrable calm of his.

The crunch of gravel announced Keert's approach.

'Ma'am, sir. Forgive the intrusion but the prime minister is on the phone.'

'Tell him you'll call him back.' Seb's narrowed gaze challenged her to do just that. 'We are in the middle of something.'

'No, we're not.' Agnesse shot to her feet. 'We're on the edge of something we *could* be in the middle of. Together. But you don't want it. Or can't even see it. You'd rather hide behind all the terrible things your family made you believe.'

She saw it so clearly now. Despite his soft kisses and tender looks, despite all his care of her, it was just duty to him. The sex was getting better and better but the real intimacy she craved was eluding her. The only thing binding them together was their unborn baby. Seb couldn't love her and he'd never really stand beside her.

She placed her hand across her belly, splaying out her fingers protectively. *In that case, we'll just have to love each other won't we, little one?* she vowed silently.

Then sent her husband the parody of a smile.

'Thank you for a lovely few minutes. But you've done your duty. I'm rested now,' she said nastily and stalked away before Seb could stop her.

Fifteen minutes.

Twenty, at most.

That was how long he'd succeeded in getting her to rest.

And then they'd fought.

As Gunter bobbed hopefully behind him, Seb remained perched at the edge of the pond, watching his wife depart.

She was dressed in a blue silk blouse and ivory linen skirt. Neat and prim. Except, as ever, for the shoes. Today it was black stilettos.

Agnesse had a fondness for vertiginous heels; Seb had developed a fondness for watching her as she moved in them. With her quick, purposeful step, the resulting sway of her pert behind always drove him just a little crazy.

Now anger was driving her; the sway was even more pronounced. He was torn between dragging her back here to finish their argument or dragging her to bed and putting an end to it that way.

He knew what she wanted from him. The same as numerous lovers had over the years. An emotional commitment. But he was never going there. He always kept that piece of himself apart. Safe. It was buried so deep he wondered if his capacity to truly feel even existed anymore.

In the meantime, she could get as angry at him as she wanted. Because he'd made no false promises. He'd married her and given her the protection of a husband. He'd saved her and the Ellamaese royal family from scandal.

And despite her ridiculous accusation that he was doing nothing here, his workload was mounting, and he was navigating that as best he could. There was no precedent for his role here, no rule book they could give to the husband of the first ever queen regnant. Particularly one who hadn't adopted any official title or duties.

Despite that, he'd received various petitions; a few of those had come from charities. He was sifting through them, deciding which he'd like to support. Others, businesses or lobbyists mostly, just wanted a piece of him so they could gain access to his wife. Those he'd deal with to ensure he stood between her and yet more pressure.

For now his main priority was to support the queen—his wife.

Again, his insides warmed at the thought of her. He could barely get used to it. The leap of his pulse when she walked into a room; the pleasure he felt when she reached out to take his hand, or even just smiled for him.

That smile was the kicker. He tried to steel himself against the effects of it, the heady mix of lust and a strange longing. She used a version of it on her people, as he'd seen Violetta do. Using a smile to bring delight to a sea of upturned faces, or charm overwhelmed staff. But the effect his wife's had on him was different. Agnesse moved him in ways he couldn't quite define. He'd convinced himself it was lust. Just lust and sexual yearning.

Nothing more. There was certainly nothing emotional behind it. He wasn't the kind of man to be *emotional* about a woman. He desired his wife.

That was all. He desired his wife and he wanted to keep her, and their unborn baby, safe.

And then, just before she disappeared from view, and as if in slow motion, Seb's entire world view was torn inside out.

Because with a bone-chilling cry and clutching desperately at her stomach, Agnesse had just sunk to the ground.

The cramping pain was so sudden and fierce she'd folded double with it. Then another wave, even more excruciating, took her legs from beneath her.

'Agnesse!' She heard Seb's panicked yell and the thundering of his feet as he sprinted towards her. She was on her hands and knees in the dirt, gasping to breathe through the agony when he reached her side.

The next hour was a horrible blur. Seb carried her inside. Yelling for doctors, for her mother. For a car. As one screeched to a halt in front of the palace entrance, he climbed in still clutching her tight to his chest. He held her, his cheek against her hair, telling her over and over it was going to be okay, all through the short drive to the private hospital on the outskirts of the city.

Where they took her away from him. When all she wanted was to cling to him and never let go. Because she knew what was happening. Everything was about to change.

She was losing their precious baby.

CHAPTER THIRTEEN

THEIR PRECIOUS LITTLE BLIP, that precious new life.

Their baby.

Gone.

Agnesse lay huddled on the bed, her faced turned away from them all as the doctors gave her the worst news.

They were so sorry, they said; there was nothing to be done. These things happened but there was no reason she and her husband couldn't have a healthy pregnancy in the future.

'See, darling,' said her mother tearfully, chaffing her hand. 'It's going to be fine.'

She ached for that tiny bundle of life that had been too fragile to survive. And she ached for the father of their little blip. The man who hid his true self behind a mask, who stood when she entered the room, and who watched her with haunted eyes. And only poured his heart into the music his mother had loved.

'No, Mama, it's not.'

She'd dared to believe she could have some part of a normal life. A man to love, a child, a family of her own. Now fate was punishing her in the cruellest of ways.

Because the loss of that precious little life had taken even more with it.

She wasn't good enough to be queen. She was barely coping with her workload. And she wasn't even good enough to keep their baby. How, then, could she hope to hold on to Seb when he didn't even want a royal life? He'd *never* wanted this. He'd only married her for their baby's sake.

Now there was no baby, why would he stay?

There was no point in protracting the agony when it was all futile anyway. Better to get it over with and push him away before he left of his own accord. She was the queen, after all. She could make that choice.

Feeling too numb even for tears, she sat up, pulled the bed covers neatly over her legs, and stiffened her spine.

'Mama, will you ask Seb to come in now please?'

They'd sent him away, out into the waiting room.

When she'd asked for her mother, not him, Seb had been too distraught to insist otherwise. Because he thought history was repeating itself, that he was losing Agnesse: like his father had lost Fabienne.

And then Mathilde had come for him and the expression on her face told him his worst fears had come true.

'Agnesse will be fine, but I'm so sorry, Sebastien, the baby is gone.'

He barely heard the rest, something about a perfectly healthy pregnancy next time. Next time? There was only one thought in his head now.

He'd failed.

His one task was to keep Agnesse and their baby safe and he'd failed. His child was lost.

'Seb?' Mathilde had to get his attention by tugging at his sleeve. 'I said she's asking for you. But be gentle and make allowances, won't you? She's not quite herself. It's been a terrible shock for her.' She placed a palm tenderly to his cheek. 'For you both.'

He nodded and set off for the room where they'd taken his wife. In the corridor the walls were lined with large framed photographs. Restful images of gardens and wildflower meadows, filled with cornflowers and daisies. Seb stared straight ahead.

Christina hovered outside Agnesse's door and closed it behind him once he had crossed the threshold, giving the queen and her husband privacy. Not, he soon discovered, that it was required. There were to be no tearful embraces, no mutual comfort for their grief at the loss of a baby.

Instead, Agnesse sat calm and still in the bed, leaning against several plumped cushions. Her expression was haughty and cool, like she was granting an audience to an unwelcome stranger. He took a bewildered step forward.

'No. Don't come closer.' She swept a crease from the counterpane. 'As you hadn't accepted the position of consort you had only one reason for being here. One purpose for being part of this family. To be the father of my child. That's done now so El-lamaa no longer has need of you.'

Be gentle, Mathilde had said. Agnesse certainly wasn't being. She landed blow after blow on him.

'But we're married,' he said. 'The loss of our child doesn't change that.'

A flicker of pain flashed through her blue eyes but was swiftly mastered. She lifted her chin and stared down her nose at him.

'It changes everything. With the baby gone what reason could there be for you to stay? From the start you've made it clear this isn't the life you ever wanted.'

He opened his mouth to answer but he couldn't summon the words to contradict her. Not when he'd confessed to precisely that only an hour or so ago.

She smiled at him, a cheerless, condescending lift of her lips. 'I'm setting you free, Sebastien.'

The use of his full name was a knife plunged into his chest. With her next remark she grabbed the hilt and twisted the blade so it slashed right through his heart.

'And I want a divorce,' she said.

He reeled. He should say something, *anything*, to fight for her, but the words wouldn't come. All he could hear was his father's taunt. *She's not for the likes of you, boy.*

'The coronation is a month away,' Agnesse said. 'I'd be grateful for your support on that day. The people deserve a celebration after a year of mourning. Once that's done you won't be needed here anymore.'

He could fall to his knees and beg her to forgive him, to reconsider, but why should she? What had he done to deserve her forgiveness?

'Very well,' he said in a flat, cold voice he barely recognised as his.

He saw her flinch, like he'd landed a wound of his own, but she quickly recovered.

'And now leave me, please.' She called for Christina and the door behind him was opened again. His audience was over.

Even in a crumpled hospital gown, her face as pale and wan as the bed sheets she sat upon, she was still more a queen than any woman he'd ever met. And he could never, ever be worthy of her.

He obeyed her without question and with a bow and a click of heels turned round and strode away.

CHAPTER FOURTEEN

HE LEFT ELLAMAA that evening. Slipping away with as little fanfare as when he and Agnesse had first arrived together. There were no pretty views to soften the pain of his departure, no graceful parkland or fairy palaces to marvel over.

No ravishing queen at his side.

He left from a deserted, private airfield in the dark of a rain-swept night and, as he had been most of his life—alone.

Leo had said there'd always be a place for him in Grimentz but Seb couldn't face the thought of being around a couple so obviously in love. So he'd spent the past month in France instead, at his father's old estate. The one the prince had purchased when he'd married Fabienne. Where Seb had been born and where his ill-fated mother was buried.

Max had inherited the bulk of their father's wealth and possessions, but along with a significant financial bequest, this Loire valley estate, with its elegant chateau and profitable vineyard, had been left to his younger brother. As if in death, Prince Georg had tried to atone for his parental failings in life.

Seb would have traded it all for a father who wanted him, but though he might never forgive him the rejection, he was at least beginning to understand his father's pain; the excruciating agony of losing the woman you loved…

Leaving Agnesse had been like tearing his still-beating heart from his own chest. Without her in it, his world was nothing.

Since he'd arrived, Seb had tried to work, but often his feet had carried him to the small cemetery in the grounds of the chateau, to where, shaded by a line of poplar trees, his mother slept, oblivious to the pain her only son was suffering. If he'd hoped to find comfort there, or answers to why fate had dealt him such blows, none was forthcoming. There was only a kinship of tragedy and heartbreak.

Leo's father had refused permission for Prince Georg's ashes to be brought here to lie with his second wife, insisting a von Frohburg should only be interred in the family crypt in Grimentz. Seb would ask Leo to reverse that decision so his parents could be reunited at last. Maybe they'd even find each other again beyond the grave.

He could grant them the happy ending their son was to be denied.

Because there was to be no such resolution for him. He would see Agnesse only one more time. He was returning to Ellamaa tomorrow to fulfil her request to support her during her coronation.

Then it would be done and he would move on. Perhaps he would come back here. This empty chateau could be put to many good uses. Whatever he did he knew he'd have to keep moving forward.

If he stopped, even for a second, the grief would crush him.

He loved Agnesse but he'd failed to protect her. His father had been right all along. Seb wasn't good enough for her. He never had been.

Perhaps it would have been better if he'd never been born, as his father had believed. Fabienne would have survived and another man would have been there to keep Agnesse safe and spare her the anguish he saw in her eyes that last day in the hospital when she'd miscarried.

The torment of that lashed him to his bones. He'd failed her. And their baby.

Seb sent up a prayer to whatever gods may be listening that his mother and father be granted peace and that his lost child, *their* grandchild, be gathered into their eternal embrace.

Then he turned away, hardened what was left of his heart, and set his course back to the realm of the living.

Seb was back.

For two final days in Ellamaa before he left for good.

He was using her father's old rooms that lay at the other end of this wing of the Winter Palace. The dowager queen had had them reopened especially for the prince, and the staff had worked tirelessly for two days solid to bring them to gleaming perfection. What a wonderful mark of respect for your husband, Dorel had gushed, as excited as all the staff seemed to be at his return.

Agnesse had offered no comment. She was merely grateful the separate stairwells meant they wouldn't accidentally meet one another in passing.

She didn't care about her mother's newfound affection for her soon to be *ex* son-in-law, or the buzz amongst the staff at the prince being back amongst them. In a matter of days divorce papers would be drawn up and this sham of a marriage would head for the courts and be brought to an end.

Before that could happen she had her coronation to get through and she'd asked Seb to be there for the sake of her people. They deserved a day of joy and happy memories. Not overshadowed by their impending divorce. Her PR team had explained away his month-long absence as matters elsewhere that had unfortunately required his personal attention.

Meanwhile, Agnesse had presented the perfect public face. She smiled serenely as she waved to the crowds, shook hands, accepted bouquets. And if she was asked where her husband was, she'd lean in and with a laugh, *Oh, you know men*, she'd say, *off saving the world or some such*. And her subjects would commiserate with her and offer their hopes for his swift return to her side.

She did what was expected and required of her, and disguised the truth of it: that it felt like pain and longing were leaking through her pores and threatening to drown her in the misery of it all.

The Winter Palace sat at the heart of the city a mile and a half from the cathedral where her coronation was to be held.

She wouldn't look at him as they attended the rehearsal walk-through together. He reached out a hand at the appropriate moments, which Agnesse never took. And which none of the clergy or staff around them had remarked on, though she saw their expressions. Compassion, sorrow, regret. Call it what you will, it made no difference. After her coronation tomorrow, Prince Sebastien von Frohburg would no longer be part of her life.

On the day, she in a gown of ivory silk, he in a uniform of a colonel of the Life Guards, she sat beside him as they'd travelled together in her carriage. Neither spoke; both kept their gazes on the crowds gathered on either side of the route. If she breathed deeper to savour sandalwood and Seb, well, she was only human. But she was required to place her hand over his as she stepped down from the carriage, and to keep it there as they processed through the cathedral, and his hand was warm and steady beneath hers at all the moments when she needed it to be.

She thought the hardest part of the day was being trapped in the carriage with him as they rode to and from the cathedral.

She'd been wrong; that moment had come later, at the coronation ball held in the glittering reception rooms of the Winter Palace. An event stuffed with the crowned heads of Europe and the great and good from around the world.

But in that sea of faces Agnesse could see only one: that of her husband's as he walked up to take her in his arms for the first dance.

The solemnity and longing in his eyes was nearly her undoing.

Agnesse sealed herself to it. She placed her hand in his. She felt need race along her spine as his other settled at her back. As supportive as ever. But she couldn't lean on him. He'd only married her because of their baby. That briefest of lives that had broken both their hearts. She couldn't doubt that. Not when she saw the sadness in his gaze. That was all for their lost child, surely.

The dance was over. He led her from the floor and towards her mother, who was deep in conversation with a dashing young man. The second son of one of Ellamaa's most high-ranking dukes.

Seb placed her hand on the young man's arm. 'I really shouldn't monopolise the queen all evening,' he said. And when he asked the queen to dance, Seb had made his farewells.

'Goodbye, Your Majesty.' He bent low over her hand, kissed her gloved fingers, and with that little heel click, was gone.

It was only after he'd gone that she realised he'd said goodbye and not good-night.

On the surface she remained as calm as ever. No

one would ever know what that cost her as inside she crumbled and broke.

She made her own farewells soon after that. Dorel was there, helping her undress, removing the tiara, the beautiful gown, the perfect heels, when her mother walked in.

'So you are still determined to push Sebastien away. Are you going to tell me why?' she said.

'It didn't work out. We can't all be as lucky as you and Papa. It wasn't a love match. He doesn't love me. And there's an end to it. I'm sorry if I've disappointed you.'

'I'm not disappointed, Agnesse. I'm angry that a daughter of mine could be so blind.'

Agnesse swung towards her. 'Didn't you hear what I said? He doesn't love me.'

'He deserves an award, then, because he's been doing an excellent impression of a man who's very much in love with his wife. Look at the photos from today, Agnesse. Look at any of the photos of the two of you since the moment he proposed to you in London. And then tell me if you feel the same.'

'I know you're wrong, Mama.'

'Am I? Then who, may I ask, sent these?' her mother asked, plucking the unopened note from amongst the bouquet of daisies that had arrived earlier that evening. 'And you haven't even read what he's written to you?' The envelope remained firmly sealed. Her mother opened the card and scanned its message. Her hand fluttered up to her breast as she gave a soft sigh. 'Well, that's really rather lovely.'

'What if he changes his mind?' Agnesse asked.

'And what if he does not?'

'I'm not good enough for him, Mama,' Agnesse said in a small voice.

'Where did you get that half-baked idea? You're the Queen of Ellamaa. You're a match for any man.' She stroked Agnesse's hair. 'I know what the problem really is. You're afraid. Everyone is when they fall in love. Because how do you bear it if things go wrong? But it's a terrible shame to let that fear prevent you from loving in the first place, darling.

'I lost your father and it crushes me every morning when I wake up and remember he is gone. But I wouldn't swap even a second of those years we had together to ease the grief I feel now. Love is precious, Agnesse. When you find it, you must grasp it with both hands.'

She kissed her cheek and placed the little handwritten card in her daughter's palm. 'And I think you should read this.'

After the door had closed behind her, Agnesse looked down, read what her husband had written to her, and felt the sting of tears forming.

Your father would have been so proud of you today.
As was I. You were magnificent.
S x

Was her mother right? Agnesse snatched up her tablet and scrolled through the photos of the day's events.

In every one, *every single one*, Seb's gaze was on her, standing at her right shoulder. When she'd paused in the portico of the cathedral, taking a moment to compose herself before she emerged into the light and her people saw their anointed queen for the first time, his hand had reached out towards her as if to steady her. It was such as small move that it would have passed unnoticed if she hadn't actually been searching the photos.

Then she searched for earlier pictures of them online. And there he was. Often a pace behind, but always with his gaze on her, fiercely protective.

Standing closer if she needed him. Giving her space if she did not.

Agnesse closed her eyes as the tears fell. All those moments, the panic attacks, the fight outside that bar, the expulsion of her mother, his endless concern and care for her? He'd been helping her, supporting her, *loving* her since that night in Vienna.

What had she done?

Agnesse dropped the tablet, abandoning the images of her loyal, steadfast husband always there, two paces behind her, and ran from her suite.

'I did not have you down as a quitter, Sebastien.'

The dowager queen had sailed into his suite without announcement while his valet was packing the last of the uniform and regalia Seb had used that day.

'Good evening, Your Majesty.' Despite her amicable tone Seb didn't, on this occasion, bother himself to bow.

'My daughter is as stubborn as they come. I thought you knew that. So why are you moping about here while she is breaking her heart over you on the other side of the palace?'

'Excuse me?'

It had taken every ounce of strength Seb had to leave Agnesse in the arms of another man. He'd wanted to drag her away, to keep her safe. She'd looked so defeated and alone and he could hardly bear it. But she'd barely spoken to him since he'd returned. It was abundantly clear how she felt about him. Yet still, the dowager queen expected *him* to go to *her*?

'It's her choice,' he said, handing the valet an item for stowing. 'She sent me away, remember?'

Mathilde waved a dismissive hand. 'She'd just miscarried. She was fighting with grief and a maelstrom of hormones. And you, Sebastien, are quite dazzling, you know. Her father was the same. I was so in awe of him it took months for me to believe he hadn't just proposed because of who my family was.'

Seb was stunned by that confession. Incredulous. There'd been a time when Mathilde was anything other than the formidable woman he knew.

She looked him up and down with a shake of her head.

'I wonder if there's ever been a female who truly thought she was good enough for you. Agnesse certainly doesn't. Once she lost the baby, she thought she had nothing else to offer you.' She made for the door again. 'Perhaps you might think about that before you leave tonight.'

And then she was gone almost as quickly as she'd arrived. Leaving Seb rooted to the spot and almost laughing at the incomprehensible suggestion that Agnesse was not good enough for him.

When the exact and polar opposite was true.

A message arrived that his car was ready. His valet was to finish what was left of his packing and follow on later. There was nothing more to keep Seb here…except his feet wouldn't move.

He had run out of reasons to see her. Tonight had been the last time he'd have her in his arms, and the realisation was a dead weight crushing his chest.

Mathilde was mistaken. His wife didn't want him. If she was breaking her heart it had nothing to do with him.

Did it?

It made no difference. He'd had his chance to protect her and he'd failed.

At last, his feet obeyed and carried him from the room.

Seb had deliberately left her in the arms of another man tonight. And he'd chosen carefully. The second son of a duke, handsome, connected, and gazing at Agnesse like she were Aphrodite herself. But would he have had any more success preventing the miscarriage once fate itself had decided that the tiny life was too fragile for this world?

Even the doctors couldn't prevent that. No one could have.

He reached the head of the staircase leading to the palace entrance. Seb grasped the banister, worn smooth by centuries of use. How many had leant on it for support, trusting implicitly in its strength as they went about their lives?

Who could do more than that? Offer their strength to another, day after day. But still, people must have fallen on these steps. One could take all the care in the world, but accidents happened.

Beyond the portico Seb could see his car. His driver and security team stood close by, waiting his arrival. They were the best at what they did and yet, that night in London he'd ended up battered and bruised. It was impossible to protect someone entirely from life. But it didn't mean you weren't good enough.

His father had loved his young wife. He couldn't have loved her more yet still, she'd died. Violetta had suffered two miscarriages before this latest pregnancy. Leo hadn't been able to prevent those, either. But he'd been there for her. Seb had seen for himself how she had leant on her husband and taken great comfort from him. Could he be there like that for Agnesse?

But would she let him?

The driver held the car door open and Seb slid into the backseat. His team took their places in the motorcade and the palace gates swung open.

No man could love her more and wasn't that what she needed in the end? Someone to love her for who she was. Not the queen, but the woman.

The engine purred to life and began to pull away.

He could do that. Surely, he was more than up to that. Agnesse was still his wife. He loved her. His world was nothing without her in it.

Agnesse. *Agnesse*...

Seb yanked his seat belt loose, reared up in his seat, and slammed his fist hard against the roof of the limousine.

'Stop the car!'

As she burst through the door to her father's old room, Seb's valet was zipping up a garment carrier. She recognised the uniform that Seb had worn earlier today.

Near the door sat a collection of luggage. An attaché case on top of the pile. Somehow, that hurt more than anything. The evidence that he'd worked here. The efforts he'd made for her. For her family, for her people.

It broke her heart all over again. How had she

mistaken what he'd been doing these past months? How had she got it so badly wrong?

That pile of luggage, so recently unpacked, was on the move again with its itinerant prince. And where would he go? Who would be there for him, comfort him, *love* him? She couldn't let any of that happen without trying to stop him.

'Where is my husband?' She didn't even try to keep the desperation from her voice.

'I'm sorry, ma'am. But Prince Sebastien has already gone.'

'Gone?' Was she already too late?

'He was heading for his car but he's only left a few moments ago. You might catch him if you hurry.'

The last of that was said into thin air. Agnesse had already spun on her heel and flown back out of the suite.

She tore along corridors and to the grand staircase leading to the exit they'd used earlier today. Framed by the looming darkness of the night sky, a black car glittered dully in the lights spilling from the portico. And it was pulling away.

Stricken, Agnesse cried out. 'Seb! No!'

Then miraculously, the car halted. She flew down the stairs, wild with relief as the back door opened and her husband climbed out.

'Seb!' She sobbed, running towards him.

The sight of the queen, arriving in a state of some agitation—actually sprinting full pelt to-

wards them—and in an even more startling state
of undress, her hair streaming loose behind her, her
dressing gown flapping open to reveal bare thighs
and sleep shorts, was the unequivocal cue for the
servants and security team to look away. That, and
the sudden and electrifying focus of the prince as
she skidded to a halt before him. Though several
sideways glances were aimed at the couple and at
least one 'About time,' was muttered.

'Agnesse.'

He didn't bow or use her title and that gave her
hope. That, and the fact his eyes were devouring
her whole. In a dark suit and white dress shirt he
was dressed almost as he was when he'd helped
her through that panic attack. He'd been helping
her pretty much ever since. How had she not seen
it? How had she not understood and valued him for
the extraordinary man he was?

'Don't go yet. I have things to say to you.' She
gathered her courage. 'What if I asked you to stay?'

'It would depend on your conditions.' he said.

That you love me. But she couldn't ask for that.
Not yet. He had to hear the words from her first. He
had to know how precious he was to her.

'I have no conditions. Because it's quite simple.
I know I can't do this without you.'

His warm gaze settled on her. 'Yes, you can. You
have been doing it without me all along.'

Drat the man for choosing now to be picky about
details.

'But I'll do it so much better with you by my side.' It was time for a grand gesture to prove her sincerity. She sank to her knees. Yes, both of them. This man deserved it.

'Marry me,' she said.

There was a murmur in the shadows around them, and from the corner of her eye she was quite certain she saw her butler punch the air.

'You do know it's just one knee for proposals?' her husband said.

She reached up to grasp his hands in hers. 'Take it as a measure of my devotion that I've used both.'

'And we're already married.'

She lifted his hands to her lips and with great solemnity pressed a kiss to both of them in turn. 'Yes, but that's just bodies and minds. I want your heart, too.' She took a deep breath. It was now or never. She had to declare herself. 'Because I love you.'

Now there was a chorus of 'ahs.' And coming from Seb's decidedly burly, and usually taciturn, security detail no less.

'Greedy girl,' he said, lifting her to her feet, gathering her in his arms and kissing her.

Yes, she was, and she was done with hiding it. 'When it comes to you I'm finding I can't get enough. I love you,' she said. 'This is me being spontaneous. Ripping up the rules and going after what I want. In this case, the man I love.' She gazed up at him. 'Very much.'

He buried his face in her hair. 'I'll confess I

wasn't leaving. I was coming back. To persuade you to give us another chance. Because I know I can't live without you. I love you and I want it all. Everything I could possibly have with you. Any title you care to bestow. Any work you want to give me to take the pressure off you. Every night falling asleep with you and every morning waking up with you in my arms.'

'You'll be my consort?'

'God, yes,' he said, sealing that promise with a kiss.

'I don't have much else to offer.'

'Are you crazy? Getting the chance to grow old with you is gift enough, *chérie*, but you've also given me a family who seems to like me, and whom I can actually stand. Yes, even Isobel, though she'd try the patience of a saint. And somewhere to truly belong. That's not something I ever thought I'd have.'

She smiled up at him. Marvelling at the unmistakable joy in his green eyes. 'You love me, then.'

'Body, soul, mind. Heart. I'm all in, *chérie*.'

She chewed her lip and buried her face in his shirt front. 'Children?' she asked.

'Yes, that, too. A palace filled with them. As many as you want. I'll love every precious one of them. As I will their beautiful mama.'

'Well, then, that's a deal. Though maybe we could wait a year or so for babies. To have some time, just for us first. Although in the meantime…'

She gazed up at him from under her lashes, slid her fingers through his and started for the stairs. 'There's nothing to say we can't have lots of *practice* at making babies.'

He sent her a positively filthy smile. 'My darling wife, I think you've just read my mind.'

EPILOGUE

Agnesse's second Anniversary Day parade was going perfectly. Ellamaa's flag flew from every vantage point, bunting festooned private homes and businesses alike, and crowds, ten deep, had cheered their queen's progress along the entire route from the cathedral, where a service of thanksgiving had been held, to the Winter Palace at the very heart of the capital. Even the weather was being kind; the sun shone from a clear, blue October sky, showing the city at its best.

Agnesse rode through the streets in a State Landau. Her mother by her side and Isobel opposite. In a guardsman's uniform, and part of her military escort, Carl was on horseback to her left. Other family members and dignitaries, including Leo and Violetta, followed in farther carriages.

With a jangle of harness and the clatter of hooves, the mounted cavalry at the head of the procession were already passing through the palace gates. The formal celebrations for the second anniversary of her coronation had nearly concluded. Only the balcony appearance awaited.

And Agnesse would be doing that alone.

Seb had told her last night that he wouldn't join her. For the second year in a row.

Despite her protestations he'd also refused to join

her in the open carriage, but at least this year he'd agreed to ride alongside as part of her mounted honour guard.

As much as she'd have appreciated the comforting presence of his solid bulk beside her, the spectacle of her prince consort, in full military regalia and astride a great black horse, was quite the compensation. The sun glinted off his gleaming gold breastplate; the horsetail plume of his spiked helmet fluttered in the breeze. Between doing her duty and waving to her subjects, Agnesse sneaked lustful glances at him again and again.

Along the route there were excited shouts for her and her family. Isobel beamed at the crowd, sending them cheery waves. Perhaps Carl sat taller in his saddle, but otherwise maintained his martial countenance. Then the spectators worked out the identity of the other rider flanking her carriage.

'Prince Sebastien!'

'We love you, Prince Sebastien.'

Agnesse shot her husband a swift look but his gaze remained fixed forward, and the only betrayal of any tension was his horse becoming restive. It pranced sideways for a few paces as if the gloved hand controlling the rein had tensed. But Seb was an experienced rider and his mount was swiftly back under control.

She wasn't surprised by the crowds adulation. Seb had won the admiration of many in the past twenty-four months. He wouldn't have it, of course.

He believed he delivered nothing more than basic royal patronage and charitable support. What those organisations actually got was a tireless campaigner and a charismatic royal ambassador. He gave his heart to anything he took on and she couldn't have adored him more. Neither, it seemed, could her people.

The carriage arrived at the palace courtyard where Agnesse alighted. With her mother and sister she took the stairs that led to the upper floor. But as she ascended she felt the onset of a warning breathlessness. This hadn't happened in a while and when it had, Seb had been there to lean on. But he was still caught up in the dismount of the honour guard.

She tried to focus on her guests who'd also left their carriages and were joining her in the salon—and not its open French windows and the grand balcony beyond. But Agnesse couldn't help it. She eyed it with growing disquiet. The numbers below were swelling as more and more of her subjects poured into the square before the Winter Palace.

Seb arrived. Minus his gold cuirass and helmet but looking no less magnificent in a scarlet tunic. She wanted to run at him and hide her face in his chest. A handful of times in the past two years when she'd nearly had an episode, he'd pulled her back from the brink. Usually just by talking. Once…well, she still blushed to think about how he'd achieved that.

Instead, she stood still and sent him a tight smile. He strolled towards her, greeting guests on the way, but she could see the concern in his cool green gaze.

He bent his head to kiss her cheek.

'Chérie,' he whispered. 'Do you need a moment?'

He understood her well enough by now. He saw the signs and always helped her deal with these now-rare moments of anxiety.

'Yes,' she breathed. Her heart was racing, her hands clammy. The day had gone well but that crowd outside was getting bigger by the minute. Perhaps it was the sheer numbers, because she was daunted by the weight of their expectations.

Seb quietly took charge. 'If you'll excuse us, the queen would like to freshen up before her appearance. You know how our ladies are,' he said pleasantly to their nearest guests, and placing a comforting hand in the small of her back, guided her towards a small retiring room that sat on one side of the salon. A place specifically designed for the monarchs to use before those iconic balcony moments. He ushered her in.

Agnesse paced nervously to the centre of the room. 'I'll be fine. I know I just need to breathe.'

'It's all right, *ma chérie,*' Seb said, coming closer. 'I know exactly what you need.'

From the look in his eye Agnesse saw instantly what he intended and backed away from her advancing husband.

'No, not that. Not here…surely.'

Her behind landed against something solid.

A previous monarch had installed a wooden vanity unit, with a porcelain sink painted with elaborate sprays of roses and trailing ivy.

Seb spared the frivolous decoration a passing glance. 'One of your forebears might have been fond of their fancy porcelains but I'm grateful. This, however—' he placed his hands on the table, trapping her between them '—is the perfect height.' With a nudge of his hips he pushed her back so she was trapped between him and its edge.

'I have the perfect way to make you relax,' he said with a wicked grin.

'We couldn't possibly. There really isn't time.' She was breathless for a whole different reason now.

His green eyes flashed.

'We both know I can make you come in three minutes flat. And nothing is guaranteed to relax you quicker,' he said, hitching up the long, full skirt of her dress with his fingers.

She placed a hand to his chest. Not to push him away, she was already beyond that, but for the pleasure of touching him.

The Royal Regiment of Horse Guards, who'd been without their Colonel-in-Chief since the death of her father, had recently asked if her husband might take on the role. She'd persuaded him to accept.

For many, *many* noble reasons.

But mostly she'd done it for the pleasure of seeing him decked out in his scarlet tunic, shiny black boots, and skin-tight riding breeches that showed off his taught backside and long, muscular legs to perfection.

She was a terrible woman, shallow and obsessed, and may the gods strike her down for using her power so frivolously, but Seb was hot, hot, *hot* in that uniform. As he sank to his knees before her she nearly climaxed there and then.

His hands slid beneath the hem of her dress and up her thighs. Thumbs hooked in the sides of her panties and peeled them down to her ankles. He supported her as she stepped out of them. Then his head and shoulders disappeared beneath her dress. One of her feet lifted from the floor as he shifted her weight to part her thighs. And then his mouth was…*oh*.

Right there. Doing to her what only Seb could do.

Agnesse no longer cared about the size of the crowd gathering outside. Only that the lace curtains at the windows were obscuring the view in. Though what would anyone actually see? The queen, looking a little flushed, leaning against a vanity unit.

Two and half minutes later she stuffed a fist in her mouth and stifled her moans as best she could. Her family and guests were gathered just on the other side of a dividing wall.

Seb reemerged. Rose up before her and made use of that pretty little basin and its scented soap.

He dampened a washcloth and collected a towel to bathe and pat her dry. When he was done she went to scoop up her panties but he got there first. But instead of handing them over to her, he stuffed them in the front of his tunic.

Her mouth fell open. 'You wouldn't dare.'

He chuckled. 'I think this will focus your mind on things other than the size of the crowd out there.' And before she could stop him he'd opened the door so they could rejoin their family and guests.

Just hidden from view of the crowds below, Seb tucked a stray lock behind the ear of his flushed and thoroughly beautiful wife.

'Right, you have your public to meet.'

'I presume you still won't join me.'

'Correct.'

Her delectable mouth formed into a frustrated pout. 'Why do I have to go out there and you get to stay in here?'

'Because they don't want me. They want you.'

'Are you sure about that? Because I heard several shouts for you on the way here.'

He'd heard them, too, but they meant nothing. A fan here or there did not mean acceptance by the wider public. He'd taken the title of Prince Consort to support his wife, not for his own aggrandisement. And he wasn't risking any balcony appearance. That was for his queen.

He swatted her on the backside. 'What are you waiting for? Get out there, woman.'

She shot him an affronted look but nevertheless smoothed her gown and, he'd swear, grew by about three inches before sailing through the doors to the roar of the crowd below.

There was a soft snuffle from behind him. He swivelled round to see Isobel approaching with a baby in her arms.

'Here's Papa's best girl,' he said, collecting the infant from her aunt's arms and settling her in his own. Green eyes, that he liked to believe were just like his, focused up on him.

Her Royal Highness, Crown Princess Fabienne-Mathilde, three-month-old future Queen of Ellamaa, gurgled and cooed and worked her tiny rosebud mouth into a smile. And stole her besotted papa's heart all over again.

Her godparents approached, Leo and Violetta, carrying their own twenty-two-month-old daughter.

Isobel smirked. 'What happens in about seventeen years and these two are grown up and the playboys of Europe come calling?'

'That's evil,' Violetta laughed. 'You're frightening their doting papas. I'm sure both our daughters will be very sensible and heed their fathers.'

'I'm sure they'll do nothing of the kind,' Isobel taunted. 'Look at who their mothers are.'

Leo and Seb exchanged panicked looks.

'That's it,' Leo said to his daughter. 'You're grounded until you are at least thirty.'

Seb gave his daughter a little sway.

'And there won't be any men allowed near you, will there?' he said to his enchanted baby in a singsong voice.

Isobel snorted. 'Yeah, right. Like you'll have any choice. Just you wait.'

It could wait because that was all a long way off. As were her royal duties.

For now she wouldn't be making any balcony appearances. That was a job for her mama and grandmama, her aunt and uncle. Today she belonged only to her parents, to her family, and their friends. A lifetime of service was yet to come. But when it did she'd have him beside her. Every step he'd be there. Till the end of his days.

As would her mother.

He watched from the shadows as Agnesse waved from the balcony. Ten minutes ago she'd practically been in bits. Now there she stood, smiling, calmly acknowledging the cheers of her people like the queen she was.

While wearing no underwear.

God, how he loved this mighty woman.

Outside, the cheering had formed into a chant. One he'd never heard before. One that caused his chest to tighten in alarm.

'We want Seb!'

'We want Seb!'

Mathilde came to his side and scooped her grand-daughter into her arms.

'Your methods might sometimes be unconventional.' She frowned at his jacket where a speck of ivory lace peeked out. Seb quickly stuffed it out of sight.

'But you've been good for my daughter, and for Ellamaa.' She looked to where Agnesse stood alone on the balcony. 'And now the people want to acknowledge you for it. So it's time to get out there.'

The chant was getting louder.

'We want Seb! We want Seb!'

But Seb was frozen to the spot. They couldn't mean it. Surely?

Violetta smiled encouragingly and Leo slapped him on the back. 'Go on,' his cousin said, giving him a shove. 'Or by the sounds of it we'll have a revolution on our hands.'

On shaky legs, Seb reached the step that led from the shadowy protection of the salon to the world outside. As he emerged into the light, the chant became louder. He reached Agnesse's side and she took his hand and kissed it. When she raised it aloft, presenting him to the crowd, a great roar went up.

Seb stood there, like a rabbit in the headlights. Where were the boos, the looks of disapproval?

'We love you, Prince Sebastien,' came a shout from the front of the crowd.

'It's okay to wave, you know,' Agnesse said, laughing. 'In fact, it's actively encouraged.'

He shot a jerky hand upward, and another roar went up. He stared out at the swirling, excited crowd below, to thousands upon thousands chanting his name.

His name. The people were cheering for *him*.

Agnesse's smile was pure sunshine. 'Breathe, my darling,' she said.

And he did.

As the terrible, twisted belief that his father had instilled in him shattered like smashed glass, Seb's chest expanded. Like he was breathing in fully for the first time—just as a new cry went up. A demand from the people to their prince consort.

'Kiss her! Kiss her! Kiss her!'

He and Agnesse had deprived the public of a balcony kiss with their private wedding.

'To hell with it. If they want Seb, they'll get Seb.'

He slipped his arm about her waist and looked to the crowd expectantly, hamming it up.

They screamed in excitement.

He tugged her closer. Another look to the masses below.

'Kiss her,' came the cry.

'Okay, hold on to that sexy little hat, *chérie*, because I'm coming in.'

As he swept her backwards, Agnesse's hand flew up to steady her flower-bedecked fascinator. She narrowed her eyes. 'I can see I'm going to have to take you in hand later.'

'Oh, Your Majesty, such promises. I can hardly wait,' he breathed. Then, as he gazed into the eyes of the woman he adored, the balcony and the red carpet beneath his feet and the crowd beyond simply went away. It was just him and Agnesse.

'I love you,' he told her. 'My beloved queen, I'm yours to command forever.'

She reached up to hook her fingers in his tunic and tugged him closer. 'In that case, to stop that crowd growing ugly, will you please get on with kissing me?'

And with a grin, and to the roars of a crowd gone wild with delight, he bent his head and obliged her.

* * * * *

Did you fall head over heels for Rivals at the Royal Altar? *Then you're sure to love these other dazzling stories from Julieanne Howells!*

Desert Prince's Defiant Bride
Stranded with His Runaway Bride

Available now!